M.J. Bikie Meets the Loch Ness Monster

by Neil Cockburn

M.J. Bikie Meets the Loch Ness Monster

Copyright © 2021 Neil Cockburn

www.mjbikie.co.uk

info@mjbikie.co.uk

Illustrations: Brian Lee
Copyright © 2021 Neil Cockburn

ISBN: 978-1-5272-8918-5

To my son Jamie and my daughter Sarah

Without whom I would never

have put pen to paper

Malcolm James Bikie dismounted his bike and carefully rested it against his highly polished desk. He brushed the snow off his heavy bearskin coat and slumped down into the comfortable swivel chair in front of his computer. Warm air pressed into his cold pale skin as he pared off his heavy woollen jumper and cast it to one side. Reaching into his desk he drew out a small ornate, bone-handled mirror. A tired face stared back at him as he peeled off his false moustache. He leaned forward and tapped some instructions into the computer before studying the screen:

The Royal Canadian Air Force have located a distress beacon on the Polar Ice Cap. The signal is believed to be that of the group of Polar explorers who went missing two days ago. A full-scale recovery mission is now under-way.

Soon the headlines around the world would be about a mysterious man who had appeared from nowhere, built shelter and set up that distress beacon, then disappeared back into the raging artic storm without trace.

Mr Bikie yawned and looked at his watch. It was three-thirty in the morning local time. Just enough time to catch a few hours sleep before he was due to take his family on holiday. Two fabulous stress free weeks of holiday he thought to himself!

CHAPTER 1

ALL ABOARD

"Let go! Let go!" screamed Spindle, as she wrestled furiously with her elder brother Sprocket.

"It's not yours. It's mine!" protested Sprocket.

"Tis not it's mine. Let go, let go!"

The small tadpole net, which was the focus of the dispute, swung around the interior of the car dangerously. As they fought for possession, Scottie, the family dog, started to bark excitedly; adding to the commotion and rowdy behaviour in the back seat of the car.

Mrs Bikie, who until now had been sitting quietly in the front passenger seat, could take it no longer. "Right that's it!" she said reaching for her seat belt. "Stop the car. Let me out. I'll walk from here!"

"Will you two please stop fighting!" shouted Mr Bikie from the driver's seat. "Hand that net over to your mother, and if there's any more trouble from you two I'm going to cancel the whole holiday!"

There was a groan of resignation as the object of the disturbance was handed over to Mrs Bikie and she quickly tucked it away down the side of her seat. Sprocket and Spindle settled back in their seats and glared at each other.

"Are we nearly there?" asked Spindle after a few minutes.

"We certainly are," replied her father, "you'll see Inverness coming up over the next hill."

Spindle leaned forward between the two front seats to get a better view and peered out of the front window. Sprocket joined her and they jostled for position.

Sure enough, as they came over the brow of the next hill, stretching out before them was Inverness the capital city of the Highlands. Only the tallest buildings and church spires were visible that day, reaching out of the early morning mist that had shrouded the city in a silky white veil.

"I'm hungry," complained Sprocket, "are we going to stop for breakfast?"

"Yes," chuckled Mr Bikie, "we're going to stop off at Jenny's Café before we go to the boatyard."

Scottie's tail started to wag vigorously at the very mention of Jenny's Café. It could mean only one thing, a special treat for him. He didn't have long to wait.

"Jenny's Café," announced Mr Bikie as he pulled off the main road into the car park.

As soon as they came to a stop Sprocket leapt out of the car and leaned back in through the open window to taunt his younger sister.

"Last one in is a 'hairy kipper'," he said, before darting off across the car park towards the café.

"That's not fair," protested Spindle, as she struggled with the door handle. "It's not fair."

"Don't worry dear," said Mrs Bikie soothingly, "he's just trying to annoy you." She lowered her voice in a conspiratorial manner as Mr Bikie stepped out of the car. "Anyway, if we get there first, your father will be the last one in!"

"Yes," said Spindle, perking up almost immediately. And with that she managed to open the car door and shot off across the car park in pursuit of her elder brother with Scottie bounding along beside her.

Mr Bikie politely opened the café door for Mrs Bikie before entering the café himself. As he stepped over the threshold he was greeted with a chorus of *"You're the hairy kipper! You're the hairy kipper!"* from the giggling children.

Jenny welcomed them all warmly and ushered them to a window table. They were soon tucking into a hearty breakfast and Scottie was given not one, but two very tasty sausages to eat.

Breakfast finished, they turned their attention to the view out of the window. From its vantage point, Jenny's Café commanded spectacular views. In the foreground, reaching out from the sea, they could see the four sturdy grey steel pillars of the Kessock Suspension Bridge. Its carriageway veiled under the fleecy white cloak of morning mist that clung to the basin of the valley.

Kessock Bridge was a pivotal point for both land and sea travellers alike. On the far side of the bridge, across the low lying land of the Black Isle, lay the majestic mountains of Ross-shire, rising today into clear blue skies that held the promise of a sizzling hot summer's day to come. In the shadow of the bridge a short distance along the shoreline was the entrance to the Caledonian Canal, the destination of the Bikie family that day.

"Can you see our boat from here?" asked Spindle, pressing her face against the window.

Mr Bikie chuckled and surveyed the mist-covered city below. "No," he replied slowly, "but you see that church spire over there, the one furthest to our left?"

"Yes," replied Spindle, following his guidance.

"Well it's sort of behind that spire and round the corner of that hill a bit," he explained as best he could.

Spindle seemed satisfied with this explanation and picked away at the remnants of her breakfast contentedly. She could hardly wait to see the boat that they had hired for their holidays. They planned to travel the entire length of the Caledonian Canal from East coast to West, from their starting point at Inverness, through Loch Ness and then on to the Atlantic Ocean.

"What time do we have to be at the boatyard?" asked Sprocket helping himself to the last piece of toast and spreading it with copious amounts of butter.

"Nine o'clock," answered his mother, "but we have to go to the supermarket first to pick up some provisions. Spindle helped me to make up a shopping list earlier."

"Where is it?" asked Sprocket, inquisitively.

"I've got it," said Spindle, "and I'm not giving it to you." She glared at him defiantly and rudely stuck her tongue out at him. This infuriated Sprocket and he glared back at her menacingly.

"Now don't start fighting again you two," said Mr Bikie glancing at his watch, "We had better get going, it's after eight o'clock already!"

Ten minutes later they pulled into the supermarket car park and Spindle took the shopping list from her pocket. She laid it on her lap and with her right hand she carefully straightened out the creases. As she lifted it up for closer inspection Sprocket pounced. He grabbed the list from her hand and jumped out of the car before making a dash for the supermarket entrance.

Spindle screeched with anger and indignation. "Mum!" she protested, tears welling up in her eyes.

"Yes I know dear," said Mrs Bikie looking exasperated. "Don't worry dear, once we're in the store I'll get it back from him."

Spindle stepped out of the car and Mrs Bikie turned to speak to her husband.

"From the moment we left home this morning Sprocket has been winding Spindle up. You'll have to do something about it. If the two of them carry on like this, the whole holiday will be ruined. There will be no peace for any of us."

Mr Bikie nodded in agreement. "I'll speak with Sprocket later," he said. "Don't worry, peace will prevail, just you leave it to me."

Half an hour later, fully stocked up with provisions, they were back on the road again. It was only a short drive to the canal.

"Caledonian Canal," announced Mr Bikie as they crossed over the small bridge that marked the start of the canal system. He flicked the car's indicator to the left and turned onto the small tarmacked road that ran along one side of the canal. Soon the road began to narrow and eventually it petered out into a rough pot-holed gravel track.

"Look!" exclaimed Sprocket excitedly. "There's a canal boat over there and it's just entering that lock. Are we going to go through that lock today dad?"

"No, not that one," replied Mr Bikie, "we're not coming back in this direction. The boat hire company is further up the canal. But don't worry, we'll be passing through lots of other locks on our journey."

"Cool," exclaimed Sprocket.

"Yes, cool," mimicked Spindle sarcastically, and even Sprocket had to laugh.

"Look," exclaimed Spindle, hardly able to contain her excitement. "It's the boatyard!"

The entrance to the boatyard was marked by a rusty old metal gate, half hanging off its hinges. As they entered they could see towering above them, like giant pieces on a chessboard, various types of boats all sitting on blocks of wood and propped up by narrow metal poles. Workmen dressed in bright orange boiler suits were busily painting their exposed hulls.

Tallest of all were the yachts that looked very different out of the water than in. Their fin-shaped hulls that provided stability when afloat seemed disproportionately large when in dry dock. The scrawny metal poles that propped them up looked dangerously inadequate for the job. All of the boats looked decidedly rickety, as though they were going to topple over at any moment. Spindle read out some of their names as they passed.

"Atlantis, Sea Conqueror, Voyager One, Moby Dick... What's our boat called Daddy?"

Mr Bikie racked his brains but he could not quite remember.

"I'm not sure," he replied, "but it's not one of these. These are in here for maintenance and repair."

Mrs Bikie rummaged around in the glove box before producing some travel documents.

"It's called the *Highland Princess*," she announced.

"The *Highland Princess*," repeated Spindle dreamily. "I like that name, it's lovely."

"There!" shouted Sprocket, pointing excitedly out of his window. "There she is!"

Spindle clambered over Sprocket in order to get a better look.

"Wow!" exclaimed Spindle. "She's huge."

"Yes she is!" said Mrs Bikie. "Are you sure that's our boat?" she looked to her husband for confirmation.

"Yes. That's the one all right," confirmed Mr Bikie smiling broadly. "I asked for the biggest and best boat they had."

"Wow!" said Spindle again.

Mr Bikie pulled the car into the visitors carpark.

"I'll just go to the office and sort out the paperwork," he said before setting off towards the main building.

"Okay crew," said Mrs Bikie, "let's start unpacking the car and taking our stuff on board. Your father can get the heavy stuff off the roof rack when he gets back."

Mr Bikie had quite a lot of stuff on the roof rack, including amongst other things his hang-glider and fishing rods.

It took them almost an hour to stow away all their gear. There was not enough space below deck for the bulkier items, so Mr Bikie secured them by rope to the boat's handrail.

Sprocket continued to tease his little sister at every opportunity and it all came to a head when she came down to the galley crying. She ran over to her mother who embraced her. Mrs Bikie looked up at her husband sternly.

"OK," said Mr Bikie, taking the hint and heading up on deck to have a word with Sprocket.

After a brief conversation, Sprocket promised to stop teasing Spindle and went below to share the good news with her.

Mrs Bikie emerged from the galley smiling. "Those two are getting on down there like a house on fire. What on earth did you say to Sprocket?"

"Oh, this and that," replied Mr Bikie. "You know, 'man to man' stuff." He turned away, not wishing to be interrogated further.

"Well whatever it was it seems to have worked wonders," said Mrs Bikie, regarding him with some suspicion.

"Yes, peace and quiet at last," agreed Mr Bikie smiling. "I think we're ready to cast off now." He crossed the deck and reached up to the ships bell.

"All hands on deck!" he called, ringing the boat's bell enthusiastically. "We're ready to cast off."

Sprocket scrambled up from the galley with Spindle and Scottie hard on his heels.

"All hands present and correct Sir," declared Sprocket saluting his father in a seafaring manner.

"Okay," said Mr Bikie, "let's get the engine fired up shall we."

He pressed the start button beside the helm and the *Highland Princess* roared into life.

"Prepare to cast off," he shouted.

"Aye Aye Captain," said Sprocket, crossing the deck and jumping down onto the jetty.

"Cast off forward," ordered Mr Bikie.

Sprocket untied the head rope from the mooring-post and threw it up to his mother, who caught it and stowed it safely away.

"Cast off aft," ordered Mr Bikie. This time Sprocket threw the stern rope to Spindle.

"All aboard!" shouted Mr Bikie.

Mrs Bikie helped Sprocket back on board while Mr Bikie made some final checks. Then he pushed the thruster forward and steered the boat out into the middle of the canal.

They could not have picked a better day for boating. The mist had all but cleared, chased away by intense summer sunshine that streamed out of clear blue skies. The waters of the canal sparkled and cast shimmers of light across the white bows of the *Highland Princess* as she pulled away from the jetty.

Spirits were high on board that day. But what nobody could have known was that this would be the last voyage of the *Highland Princess* - she would never again return to these waters. Nor could they have imagined the perils and terrible danger that they would soon have to face.

CHAPTER 2

SHIP AHOY

As the *Highland Princess* settled into a leisurely glide Mr Bikie sat back in the helmsman's chair and soaked up the warm rays of sunshine. Sprocket along with Scottie went foredeck and took up position on the bow. To one side of the canal a sprawling housing estate clung to the steep sides of a hill, whilst in contrast the opposite embankment was covered with wild flowers that stretched back into the woodland beyond. Soon the houses gave way to grassy meadows and open fields.

Their first navigational obstacle lay ahead - the swing bridge that carried the main road from the city centre heading west.

"Bridge dead ahead," shouted Sprocket from the bow.

A flotilla of canal boats were huddled together waiting for the bridge to open. Mr Bikie reversed the thruster and the *Highland Princess* glided to a graceful halt at the back of the queue.

"I don't think we'll have to wait long," said Mr Bikie. "This queue looks like it's been waiting here for some time.

Soon an alarm bell alerted everyone that the bridge was about to open. Red stop lights on either side of the road-bridge flashed warning as two large red and white barriers swung down across the highway, stopping the busy summer traffic in its tracks. An enormous electric motor attached to the side of the bridge screeched into action. Steel wheels grated and rumbled along metal tracks as the bridge swivelled round into its new position.

With a signal from the Bridge Keeper, the flotilla started to make headway through the newly opened channel. Admiring onlookers on either side of the canal gathered to watch the flotilla's stately progress. A group of excited foreign tourists disembarked from one of the many waiting coaches, eager to take photographs of the event. Scottie ran around the deck barking excitedly as Sprocket waved to the assembled audience. They all waved back to him enthusiastically.

On hearing the commotion, Spindle and Mrs Bikie came up from the galley and were soon enjoying the sense of occasion.

"It's like being a member of royalty," shouted back Sprocket from his position on the bow.

The *Highland Princess* was the last boat through and as they cleared the bridge, Sprocket made his way aft to watch the great steel and concrete structure swing back into its original position. Alarm bells rang out as the chattering tourists scrambled hurriedly back to their vehicles. Soon the flashing red lights gave way to green permitting them to resume their onward journeys.

"That was brilliant!" exclaimed Sprocket. "Do we pass through any more swing bridges on our way dad?"

"Yes, I think so," replied Mr Bikie reaching down into the map box. "There's a chart in here somewhere. Yes, here it is." He handed the chart over to Sprocket and with Spindle's help he unfolded it out onto the table. Mrs Bikie looked on with interest.

"Where are we now mum?" asked Sprocket.

"I think we're here," said Mrs Bikie, stepping forward and pointing to a spot on the chart. "It looks like the next road crossing is not until we reach Fort Augustus at the bottom end of Loch Ness. That's a long way from here."

"Oh," said Sprocket, looking disappointed.

"According to this though," continued Mrs Bikie, "we have only a few miles to go before we reach our first proper canal gate, which is called," she hesitated for a moment to pronounce it correctly, "*Dochgarroch Lock*."

"Wow, a lock," said Spindle. "I can't wait to go through one of those!"

"No more swing bridges today though," sighed Sprocket. "Where do we go after that mum?"

"*Loch Dochfour*," replied Mrs Bikie. "Then it's on to Loch Ness." She pointed to a spot further along the chart.

"Loch Ness! That's where the monster lives, isn't it," said Sprocket excitedly.

"Monster?" frowned Spindle. "What do you mean Monster?"

Sprocket took no notice of her. "Will we reach Loch Ness today?" he asked turning to his father.

"Yes I expect so," replied Mr Bikie, "we should reach the castle by this afternoon."

"You mean Loch Ness Castle," said Sprocket, "where the monster lives?"

"Well it's actually called Urquhart Castle," said Mr Bikie, "and that's where the monster…"

"Mum!" protested Spindle, "Sprocket's making this up to frighten me, isn't he? There is no monster in the loch is there?" She turned to Sprocket and glared at him angrily.

"You're not supposed to tease me. Now we won't get that extra pocket money that dad promised us."

"Extra pocket money?" enquired Mrs Bikie.

Mr Bikie and Sprocket stared at Spindle, willing her not to say any more, but there was no stopping her.

"Yes," said Spindle unabated, "dad told Sprocket that if we were both good and if Sprocket stopped teasing me that we would both get extra pocket money."

Spindle stopped abruptly and covered her mouth. Sprocket had told her she wasn't to tell mum. It was their secret.

"I see," said Mrs Bikie, looking at her husband reproachfully. "So that was what the 'man to man' talk with Sprocket was all about, nothing but bribery and corruption!"

Mr Bikie made no comment and shuffled sheepishly from one foot to another. Sprocket tried to defend his own position.

"Will somebody please tell Spindle I'm not teasing her," he protested. "There really is a monster in Loch Ness, isn't there dad?"

"Well yes… there is supposed to be a monster in Loch Ness," replied Mr Bikie sceptically, "but nobody has ever proved that it actually exists."

"Well, monster or no monster," said Mrs Bikie, "I'm going down below to finish the unpacking. Come on Spindle".

And with that, she took Spindle's hand and they disappeared back down into the galley.

"Phew!" said Sprocket. "Spindle really dumped us in it there didn't she dad? About you doubling our pocket money I mean."

"Yes," replied Mr Bikie, "But perhaps it would be better not to mention the bit about doubling it!"

Sprocket nodded his head sagely in agreement before heading back with Scottie to what was fast becoming their favourite spot on the boat, the bow of the *Highland Princess*.

As the *Highland Princess* cut serenely through the calm glittering water, Scottie raised his ears to capture the warm air as it breezed by. Sprocket studied the water ahead, enjoying their stately progress along the canal. He was just drifting off into a daydream when he spotted another boat approaching fast.

"Dad!" shouted Sprocket. "That boat looks like it's heading straight for us!"

Mr Bikie, sensing the urgency in Sprocket's voice, focused his attention on the oncoming vessel. It was travelling at speed on the wrong side of the canal. Mr Bikie gave a long blast on the boat's horn in warning, but the captain of the other vessel took little to no notice and held steady on collision course.

There was a sickening thud and crunching sound as the other boat ploughed into the starboard side of the *Highland Princess* before bouncing off and continuing on its erratic course down the canal. The captain of the other boat shouted abuse in a foreign tongue and waved what looked like a bottle of wine around in the air menacingly.

"…imbécile, tu as frappé mon bateau….

Mr Bikie was about to respond, but when he looked toward the bow where Sprocket had been standing, he was nowhere to be seen.

"Sprocket! SPROCKET!" cried out Mr Bikie.

"It's alright dad, I'm here," said Sprocket coming up behind him.

Mr Bikie spun round.

"Thank goodness!" exclaimed Mr Bikie. "For a moment I thought you'd gone overboard."

Mrs Bikie and Spindle came up from below. "What's happened?" asked Mrs Bikie. "Is everybody OK?"

"Yes we're fine," replied Mr Bikie. "No thanks to that madman," he said pointing in the direction of the fast disappearing boat.

"Where's Scottie?" asked Mrs Bikie.

"Scottie?" said Sprocket looking around, "SCOTTIE!"

"THERE!" screamed Spindle, pointing back down the canal to a small black bundle of fluff in the water. "He's drowning. SCOTTIE!" she cried in distress. "Help him! Help him!"

Mrs Bikie looked over to her husband and something passed between them; something unsaid. Mr Bikie nodded almost imperceptibly as she kicked off her shoes and dived head first into the cool quivering water. She was an accomplished swimmer and they all watched admiringly as she glided through the water towards the distressed Scottie.

It had been some twenty years since she and Mr Bikie had first met. He was a young journalist and she a freelance photographer. Both had been assigned by an international magazine to cover a story about the building of a new hydro dam in the foothills of Nepal. But whilst there, they started to hear rumours about a secretive and ancient civilisation who were said to live in a hidden valley high up in the Himalayan Mountains. According to local legend, the inhabitants had mystical and magical powers and possessed technology that was far more advanced than anything existing in the West.

After completing their assignment for the magazine they decided to stay on for a while and search for the mythical secret valley. Together they found it and this had changed their lives forever!

During their time there together they had fallen deeply in love with each other and were married in the Temple of Desire, one of many opulent temples in the valley.

Together they studied and learnt the mystical ways of the people, remaining there for four years until they finally felt ready to leave the valley and return to the West.

Before leaving, they vowed never to divulge the location of the valley, nor tell anyone of its secrets.

As a parting gift, they were given a beautifully ornate wooden box containing a very special crystal. The crystal possessed powers that enabled the rightful owners to trans-locate anywhere they wanted, anywhere in the world instantly. They had both taken an oath that they would never use it for wicked or evil purposes, or for their own personal gain and enrichment.

Scottie did his best to paddle towards Mrs Bikie and she grabbed hold of him before starting back towards the boat. Sprocket untied the large landing net that was lashed with Mr Bikie's hang glider to the boat's railing and held it over the side as his mother approached. Mrs Bikie carefully placed Scottie into the open net and with Spindle's help, Sprocket managed to haul Scottie back on board while Mr Bikie helped Mrs Bikie out of the water. They all gathered around Scottie who lay motionless on the deck.

"Is he all right?" asked Spindle anxiously.

"He's not moving," said Sprocket.

"He's fine," said Mrs Bikie, "just a bit shocked I expect; he's not injured."

As she moved forward to help Scottie out of the net, he pulled himself to his feet and started to shake himself vigorously. Cold water droplets splashed out in all directions and they backed away screeching with laughter. Scottie satisfied that he was dry enough wagged his tail energetically and looked up at them gratefully. They all gathered around again and made a big fuss of him.

"Oh Scottie," said Spindle, kneeling down and giving him a big hug, "you gave us such a fright!"

CHAPTER 3

DOCHGARROCH LOCK

"We had better check for damage," said Mr Bikie. "Is everything all right below Marion?"

"Yes, I think so," replied Mrs Bikie.

"You'd better have a look at this dad," said Sprocket, peering over the side.

They all joined him and leaned over the rail. A large gash ran down the entire length of the starboard side. There was a collective groan.

"I think he may have snagged your hang glider too dad."

Mr Bikie examined his hang glider briefly, but he could see no visible damage.

"The glider seems to be OK," he said, "but the boat; well that's a different matter. We'll have to report the accident and damage to the boatyard. God knows what they're going to say."

"But it wasn't our fault," protested Sprocket indignantly.

"Let's hope the people at the boatyard see it that way," said Mrs Bikie, "or this may be the shortest boating holiday in history."

There was a collective groan from the children. Mr Bikie reached into his pocket for his phone.

"Mmm.. no signal, mobile coverage around here must be a bit patchy," he said. "We'll have to find another way to contact them."

"I think I saw a post office marked on the map earlier," said Mrs Bikie. "They'll probably have a public telephone we can use there.

Sprocket go and fetch me that chart we were looking at earlier please. It's down in the galley next to the helm."

Sprocket dashed below, returning a few moments later with chart in hand. Mrs Bikie unrolled it and spread it out onto the table.

"Yes, here," she said, putting her forefinger on the chart. "There is a post office at that place I mentioned earlier, *Dochgarroch Lock*."

"So what's our position now," asked Mr Bikie studying the chart. "How far do we have to go till we get there?"

"Well we're about here," said Mrs Bikie pointing at the chart again, so I'd say, three, maybe four miles away. But more to the point, do you think we'll be able to get the boat there? I mean, with it being so damaged?"

Mr Bikie peered over the side again. "Well," he said, "I'm no expert, but I think it will be OK."

"Let's get started then," said Mrs Bikie, folding the chart away.

It took them just under an hour to reach *Dochgarroch Lock* and as the *Highland Princess* pulled up to the jetty Sprocket jumped ashore to secure the mooring ropes.

"I'll head up to the post office and see if they have a phone," said Mr Bikie.

"We'll all go," said Mrs Bikie. "Anyone fancy an ice-cream?"

There was a chorus of 'yes' from the children and they all set off along the narrow tow-path towards the post office. They entered the store and Sprocket, followed by Spindle, ran straight to the ice cream cabinet. A slightly plump, middle-aged lady came from behind the counter to help them open the heavy sliding doors at the top of the ice-cream cabinet. She smiled broadly as she assisted them with their choice. Selection made they returned to the counter and Mrs Bikie paid for the ice creams.

"Do you have a public phone here by any chance?" asked Mr Bikie politely. "Our mobile phone doesn't seem to have a signal."

"No, I'm sorry sir, we haven't," replied the woman pleasantly. "Everybody around here's been complaining about the mobile signal. It's been like that for days. But there's an old fashioned public phone box that the locals sometimes use about a quarter of a mile from here. When you come out of here sir, follow the lane up towards the main road. You can't miss it!"

Mrs Bikie decided that she also fancied an ice-cream and bought another one for herself. They gave the lady a cheerful farewell before stepping out into the blazing hot sunshine.

"Come on Scottie," said Mr Bikie, "Let's walk up to the phone box... anyone else coming?"

"You carry on dear," said Mrs Bikie. "We'll wander back to the boat and eat our ice creams on the way. We'll see you when you get back."

They set off back along the tow-path and not far from where the *Highland Princess* was moored they found a lovely picnic table nestled under an overhanging tree. They settled back to watch as a handful of boats entered *Dochgarroch Lock*. The lock gates closed behind them and water gushed in, raising the boats to a higher level.

"I wish we were going through that lock right now," said Spindle. "We won't lose the *Highland Princess* will we mummy? I mean, they won't take her away from us, will they? They will let us carry on won't they?"

"I'm not sure dear," replied her mother, "we'll just have to wait and see what your father says when he gets back."

No sooner had she spoken than they saw Mr Bikie and Scottie coming back along the tow-path. He joined them at the picnic table and took a seat.

"Well? Did you get a hold of the boatyard?" asked Mrs Bikie. "What did they say?"

"Well," replied Mr Bikie, "they seemed to know all about the accident and the man who crashed into us. Apparently, it was one of their boats that he was hiring. They said that the police had contacted them to say that they had arrested the man for being drunk and in charge of the boat. They also said that after he hit us on the canal he went on and crashed into that swing bridge we passed through earlier. Believe it or not the idiot reversed his boat and rammed the bridge for a second time!"

"Was anyone hurt?" asked Mrs Bikie, concerned.

"It seems not," replied Mr Bikie, "but they've had to close the bridge for inspection and there are traffic jams building up for miles around. The entire city centre of Inverness has come to a halt, gridlocked by traffic. The police have had to call in reinforcements from outlying areas just to get things moving again. It's chaos!"

"What about the *Highland Princess*?" asked Spindle anxiously.

Mr Bikie frowned. "I'm not sure yet," he replied, "they said that they had an engineer in the area and that he would have to inspect her to see if we could carry on or not. I'd better go and wait for him over at the boat. They said he wouldn't take long to get here."

As Mr Bikie headed over to the *Highland Princess* a sense of gloom descended upon those left behind at the picnic table.

Sprocket looked to his mother for reassurance. "They'll give us another boat won't they mum? I mean, if we can't continue on the *Highland Princess*?"

"I expect so," replied his mother uncertainly.

Spindle was not happy. "But I don't want another boat," she said sulkily, "I want the *Highland Princess*."

It wasn't long before the man from the boatyard arrived.

"That's the man dad's been expecting," said Sprocket pointing over to the *Highland Princess*.

Mr Bikie, who had been waiting for him patiently, greeted him and they boarded the boat. They watched from the picnic table as the engineer, clipboard in hand inspected the *Highland Princess*. After ten minutes or so, the engineer shook Mr Bikie's hand and made his way back along the tow-path. Mr Bikie returned to the picnic table and sat down.

"Well?" asked Mrs Bikie. "What's the verdict?"

"He said that the damage was only superficial," replied Mr Bikie. "Nothing luckily that can't be fixed with a bit of filler and a fresh coat of paint when we return her to the boatyard."

He smiled broadly.

"So it is good news! We can all carry on!"

They all cheered with approval at this welcome news and headed back to the *Highland Princess* in high spirits.

"All aboard," called Sprocket as he unhitched the mooring ropes.

They clambered back on board and were soon negotiating the lock that Spindle had so wanted to go through. Once clear, they made good headway through a small loch named *Loch Dochfour*. The loch, wide at first, started to close in and eventually narrowed into a channel.

"Look," said Sprocket, pointing ahead. "What's that white building over there?"

"It's a lighthouse," said Spindle.

"It doesn't look much like a lighthouse to me," said Sprocket, eyeing his sister questioningly. "It looks more like an ordinary house to me, and how would you know what it was anyway?"

"Because I can read," replied Spindle sarcastically, waving a guide book in front of his nose.

Sprocket grunted.

"It's called Bona Lighthouse," continued Spindle, "and it's over 200 years old. It is also the only inshore lighthouse in Scotland."

Spindle had rattled off the facts without once referring back to the guide book. Sprocket sometimes found his little sister a bit irritating; a bit too clever for his liking.

"In the olden days," continued Spindle, having now captured everybody's attention, "the lighthouse keeper used to hang a lantern in the bay window at the front of the house, so that boats could safely find their way to the entrance of the channel at night."

"And for us," announced Mr Bikie, "the lighthouse marks the entrance to Loch Ness."

CHAPTER 4

FIRST CONTACT

The *Highland Princess* eased through the narrow channel before entering the vast expanse of Loch Ness. The loch was some twenty-three miles long, and in parts over seven hundred feet deep.

"Take the helm for me please Marion," said Mr Bikie. "I think I'll go below and make us all some sandwiches for lunch."

"I'll come and help," offered Spindle enthusiastically and they both disappeared below.

Mrs Bikie took the helm.

"When will we see the castle?" asked Sprocket.

"We have a way to go yet," chuckled Mrs Bikie, "but you'll see it soon enough.

Sprocket returned to his favourite spot on the bow and remained there with Scottie until at last he caught sight of the castle in the distance.

"I think that's the castle over there?" he called back, pointing it out to his mother.

"Yes, that's it," confirmed Mrs Bikie, "Loch Ness Castle or as your father said Urquhart Castle to give it its proper name. That's where they say the Loch Ness Monster prowls the waters. And over there," she said pointing across into the bay, "is the village of Drumnadrochit. Go and tell the others that we're arriving. Where are those sandwiches anyway? I'm starving!"

Sprocket went below and returned with the others, all keen to get their first glimpse of the famous castle. Spindle carried with her a huge platter of sandwiches.

Urquhart Castle stood dominant over the bay at Drumnadrochit. For centuries it had reigned supreme over these waters and the surrounding countryside. However, sieges over the years, particularly after the Jacobite Rising of 1689, had reduced this once mighty castle to near ruin. The pitch black reflection it cast over the loch that day, made it look especially dark and foreboding. Sightings of a monster in these waters had been reported as long ago as 565 AD.

Spindle gave an involuntary shiver as the *Highland Princess* plunged into the deep cold shadow of the castle.

"It's very scary here," she said, putting an arm round her mother's waist for reassurance, "I don't like it here! There's something bad here! Something horrible! We're not staying here are we mummy?"

"Oh don't be such a scaredy-cat," said Sprocket. "Dad said we're staying here for the next couple of days."

"We're not are we daddy?" asked Spindle, looking at her father.

"Well, yes," said Mr Bikie. "It's all arranged. Tomorrow I'm taking my hang-glider to a mountain near here called 'Carn Gorm', and I've hired the local gamekeeper to take me most of the way up in his all-terrain vehicle."

Spindle looked very unhappy. Somehow she sensed that there was some terrible danger in these waters.

"I'll tell you what," said Mr Bikie, not wanting to see Spindle upset. "I'll see if I can re-arrange for the gamekeeper to pick me up from the boat tomorrow morning and we can anchor on the other side of the loch tonight. That way, you and Sprocket can set up a base camp on the far shore tomorrow. How does that sound?"

Spindle and the others all nodded their heads in approval.

Mr Bikie reached into his pocket and took out his mobile.

"Drat," he exclaimed, "I'm still not getting a signal."

"I'll tell you what," said Mrs Bikie. "Let's all go ashore for a while. There is bound to be a public phone around here somewhere."

"What about lunch?" enquired Sprocket, looking at the huge pile of freshly made sandwiches.

"We'll take them with us," said Mrs Bikie. "I think we're all feeling a bit peckish. We can have a nice picnic somewhere."

This idea met with universal approval and Mrs Bikie steered the *Highland Princess* towards the castle pier. In no time at all they were climbing the steep path that led along the periphery of the castle grounds to the main road and visitor's centre.

There was no public phone available at the visitor centre so they decided to catch a shuttle bus to the nearby village of Drumnadrochit. When they reached the village, Mr Bikie found a bright red phone box outside the village post office and confirmed the new arrangements with the gamekeeper for the next day.

There were a number of picnic benches on the village green opposite the post office and they all settled down to eat their sandwiches.

"Well," said Mr Bikie, "We've got 'Cheese and Ham', 'Tuna-Mayonnaise' or 'Roast Beef with Arran Mustard'."

"Cheese and Ham for me," said Sprocket grabbing a sandwich. "Where're the crisps?"

"Where are the crisps... please," said Mrs Bikie opening a large bag of crisps and placing them in the middle of the picnic table.

"What would you like dear?" Mrs Bikie asked Spindle. Spindle leaned forward in her seat.

"I think I'll have Tuna-Mayonnaise please mum," she replied politely.

As Mrs Bikie handed Spindle her sandwich Scottie looked up and gave a little whine.

"Oh I'm sorry Scottie," said Mrs Bikie apologetically. "Don't you worry; I've got your favourite doggy biscuits here." She reached down into her backpack and produced a large packet of dog biscuits and a bowl. Then they all settled down to discuss what they would do for the rest of the afternoon. A visit to the 'Loch Ness Monster Exhibition' came top of the voting list, and once they had finished their picnic they set off, crossing the old stone bridge that spanned the River Enrick.

The afternoon passed quickly, and all too soon they were back on board the shuttle bus and heading back to the castle. Once there, they followed the steep path down to the pier.

"All aboard," called out Sprocket before unhitching the ropes and jumping aboard himself.

Mr Bikie took the helm this time and reversed the *Highland Princess* away from the pier before swinging the boat around and heading off across the loch.

They found a pleasant little spot on the far side and anchored in the bay about a hundred meters off shore. Soon the air was filled with the smell of cooking wafting up from the galley where Mrs Bikie was preparing the evening meal.

They were hungry again now, and when Mrs Bikie announced that dinner was ready they gathered around the dining table eagerly.

Having finished their hearty meal, Sprocket went to find a board game while Spindle helped her mother to clear away the dishes. As evening was fast approaching, Mr Bikie went up on deck to switch on the night navigation lights.

He looked out across the loch towards the west. The sun was getting low in the sky and rays of orange and yellow light streamed out from the horizon, turning the waters of the loch into a beautiful kaleidoscope of colour. High above him, small white cotton-wool clouds burst into orange as the rays caught them in their gaze. Mr Bikie sat back on one of the benches, captivated by his surroundings.

It was then that he caught sight of a flash of light in the corner of his eye. He turned and looked in that direction. There it was again, a brilliant white flash of light reflecting from something high up on the hill above the shoreline. He reached for his binoculars and panned up the steep hillside. He froze momentarily. A man stood on the brow of the hill pointing his own set of binoculars directly back at him. The sinister figure ducked down out of sight as soon as their lenses met.

Mr Bikie put his binoculars to one side and frowned. Someone was spying on him! But who? And for what reason?

He returned to the galley deep in thought. The others had cleared everything away and Sprocket had set up a game of Scrabble.

"You're just in time daddy," said Spindle, "we're just about to start."

Mrs Bikie noticed that her husband looked worried. "What is it dear? Is there something the matter?"

"No," replied Mr Bikie, shrugging the incident off. "I'll tell you about it later...now who gets first turn?"

The first game was won by Mrs Bikie, but the second game was much closer.

"Your turn Sprocket," said Mrs Bikie.

Sprocket surveyed the board.

"Got it," he cried, and began to lay out his word.

Spindle spelt it out as he laid down each tile.

"M.O.N.S.T.E.R... monster," she said.

"Like the Loch Ness Monster," said Sprocket. "That's twenty-eight points to me," he added triumphantly.

Spindle started to dutifully record his score when she suddenly paused and looked up at the others.

"Shh, listen!" she said. "I can hear something..."

Scottie could hear it too and gave a long low growl. "Shush quiet Scottie," she said.

They all fell silent, wondering what Spindle and Scottie could hear.

They felt it through the floor first, a slight tremor to begin with. Then a strange whining sound echoed around the galley getting louder and louder until it was almost unbearable. The boat started to shake and rock violently from side to side and the scrabble board they had been playing on flew off the table, scattering the letter tiles in every direction. Spindle screamed and protected her head as cupboard doors flew open, flinging out their contents, crashing and shattering all around her.

"Everyone on deck," shouted Mr Bikie, reaching under the bench seats for the life jackets. "Put these on, hurry!"

They scrambled up on deck, pulling on their life jackets as they went.

"Look!" exclaimed Sprocket pointing over the side. "Down there. Look!"

They peered over the side and were just in time to see a large black shadow disappear into the murky depths of the loch.

"It's the monster!" exclaimed Sprocket. "It's the Loch Ness Monster!"

Spindle looked frightened and held on to her mother tightly.

"We'd better get back below," said Mr Bikie. "Whatever it was it's gone now."

Later that night Mr Bikie told Mrs Bikie about the man on the hill. The man he had seen spying on him earlier that evening. Something strange is going on around here he had told her. Something strange and he wasn't quite sure what it was.

CHAPTER 5

THE MONASTERY

Lachlan McGregor, the local gamekeeper, bid him farewell and watched as Mr Bikie launched himself off the summit of 'Carn Gorm'. The early morning sun shone brightly, burning away the silky white mist that carpeted the valley below. He marvelled at his surroundings as the spectacular mountain peaks pushed themselves up into clear blue skies.

He had planned to fly west towards Loch Monar, but after the events of the previous evening all that had changed. Instead, he flew east back towards Loch Ness.

Ever since his first fleeting glimpse of the man on the hill with the binoculars it had been playing on his mind. He had been replaying the scene over and over again. There was something familiar about the figure on the hill, something that he could not quite put his finger on.

It was not long before nestled on the shores of Loch Ness Urquhart Castle came into view. Further ahead, still anchored off the far shore, he recognised the *Highland Princess* and set course across the loch towards her. As he drew closer he caught sight of Mrs Bikie standing on the deck looking out for him. She waved enthusiastically and he tilted the wings of his glider from side to side in acknowledgement. He soared over the *Highland Princess* and continued towards the hill where he had seen the man the night before.

A flattened patch of green grass near the top of the hill was evidence that someone had pitched a tent there recently, but there was no sign of the man himself. He glanced at his watch before pitching his glider sideways and heading off down the loch. He would come back later and see if the man had returned.

Less than a mile along the shore, he came across a monastery clinging to the side of the loch. No roads led to it or from it, as the banks were too steep at this point. There was a large ramshackle boathouse on the edge of the shore that looked as though some effort had been made to patch it up recently.

He swooped down towards the monastery to get a closer look and, as he did so, he saw a group of monks, all dressed in black cloaks emerging from the building. As the monks filed out of the main door they pulled their hoods up in a furtive manner and set off down the rocky path towards the boathouse.

The monk leading from the front stood out from the others. He was much taller, leaner and physically well built. But it was the monk walking a few paces behind him that drew Mr Bikie's attention. As soon as the monk spotted him, he reached under his cloak and pulled out a shiny object. The leader of the group turned and shouted something at him before striking him violently on the arm. What looked like a gun clattered onto the rocky path and the monk who had produced it quickly retrieved it and tucked it away back under his cloak.

All of the monks were now steadfastly focused on Mr Bikie and his hang glider. Mr Bikie was shocked. Why would anyone point a gun at him, let alone a monk? Monks don't go around with guns. He tipped his wings from side to side in a friendly salute, hoping that this would convince them that he hadn't seen anything. Then he completed his swoop over the monastery before turning his glider and heading back down the loch.

Then he saw something else; something that the monks would not have wanted him to see. Just below the surface of the water, coming across from the far shore was a dark menacing looking shadow. He watched it as it headed for the entrance of the boathouse before disappearing inside.

This, thought Mr Bikie, was what the monks were protecting and why his presence had so disturbed them. He knew exactly what it was now. It was the same thing he had seen the night before when the *Highland Princess* had almost been sunk. It was not a monster he was looking at. It was a submarine!

All the while, the group of monks had been tracking him with their eyes. Staring up wondering what, if anything, he might have seen. He dared not look back; he could feel their eyes burning into him. Whatever that submarine was up to it must be something of great importance to them. Something of deadly importance!

Mr Bikie carried on down the loch for a short distance before gaining height and crossing over into the next valley. This valley ran parallel to Loch Ness and enabled him to head back, all the time keeping blindside to the monastery. After a while, he turned towards Loch Ness again and swooped over the hillside above the *Highland Princess*. There was still no sign of the man with binoculars.

He picked up a rising thermal to gain height and the warm rising air lifted him higher and higher. As he circled round and round he tried to clear his mind and make sense of all that had happened recently.

He had only been on holiday for twenty-four hours and already he had been in a boat accident, been spied upon by a strange man on the hill, almost been sunk by what everyone thought at the time was the Loch Ness Monster, and now almost been shot out of the sky by that strange group of monks. Could all these things be connected in some way?

His thoughts were jolted as his gaze fell on the waters of the loch below. Once again he spotted the black shadow of the submarine, this time heading up the centre of the loch. He watched as it turned towards Urquhart Castle.

Well, thought Mr Bikie, whatever was happening around here, it looked as though he was now part of it. He decided to pursue the shadow and put his glider into a steep dive.

It was then that things went really badly wrong. He heard a tearing sound above him and looked up in alarm. The canvas of his glider was beginning to tear away from its frame; a jagged piece of aluminium tubing protruded out of the front where canvas should have been. He thought back to when the *Highland Princess* had been involved in the accident and remembered that Sprocket had said that the glider might have been damaged. He cursed himself for not paying greater attention.

The glider was becoming unstable, veering to the left, then to the right, before starting to spiral down out of control. Mr Bikie looked around desperately for a place to land. The grassland to the south of the castle looked like his best bet, but the glider had taken on a will of its own. The castle walls loomed large as he fought desperately to regain control. A small boy standing on the castle battlements with his mother looked up as he approached.

"Look mummy. That man is heading straight for us and he's going to crash!"

An involuntary scream welled up in the back of Mr Bikie's throat as he headed towards the castle wall.

He managed to clear the top of the wall with inches to spare and whizzed passed the little boy and his mother screaming.

"Some sort of madman," said the little boy's mother dismissively "Now come away Wee Johnny, we have to get back to the hotel for our breakfast."

Johnny looked at his mother in earnest. "But I think that that man was in some sort of trouble mummy. He looked as though he was going to crash!"

"Nonsense," replied his mother, "now come away Wee Johnny. I'm not paying that hotel good money for breakfast and missing out on it! Especially not for the sake of some sort of lunatic flying man in a hang glider!"

CHAPTER 6

MCTAVISH'S ANGEL

Mr Bikie overshot the castle and careered headlong towards the forest at the far end of the castle grounds. He made a futile running motion with his legs as he encountered the top canopy of the trees. But the trees soon devoured him, flaying his body with their branches before bringing him to an abrupt and sickly halt.

Battered and bruised, but still alive, Mr Bikie was left dangling halfway up a tree, still some thirty feet off the ground. He looked around and took stock of his situation. Above him, his wrecked glider had snagged itself on a branch; at least he wasn't going to fall any further.

That woman, the one that he had seen on the castle battlements with the little boy, she would have seen him crash. There would be somebody along to help him soon.

Half an hour turned into an hour, but still, no one came to his aid. He looked at his watch. It was just after nine o'clock in the morning. Tourists would be arriving at the castle in droves by now, he would just have to swallow his pride and call out for help. He called out several times but to no avail. Crows started to assemble around him on nearby trees, like vultures waiting for their next meal. More crows were arriving all the time.

He decided that he would have to take his chances and unbuckle himself from the hang glider before free-falling to the ground. A few broken bones might be the price he would have to pay for his freedom.

He surveyed the ground below. What sort of landing could he expect? There was a large rock just off to one side with a badger sett at its base. Thankfully he would miss that. Directly below him, the forest floor was covered by a mixture of heather and moss. Could be worse, he thought to himself.

He was building up the courage to release his harness when he heard a sound below. It seemed to be coming from the hole under the big stone. He focused his attention on the opening and strained to hear. Yes, it was definitely coming from there.

To his astonishment an old man crawled out of the hole and stood up to look around.

"Up here!" called down Mr Bikie, relieved to see someone at last.

The old man looked up to where Mr Bikie was dangling.

"Ah there you are," he said in a strong Scottish accent. "I've been expecting you. Wait there and I'll have you down in a jiffy, just give me a wee minute."

With that, the old man disappeared back down the hole, leaving Mr Bikie to puzzle out the man's words. What did he mean when he had said that he was expecting him? How could he be expecting him? And what was he doing down that hole anyway?

After a short time, a ladder started to emerge from the mouth of the hole. It kept coming and coming until the last rung had cleared the entrance. The old man followed the ladder out and sat on the big rock for a moment to catch his breath. Then with no small effort, he swung the ladder high up against the tree, beyond the point where Mr Bikie was hanging.

Mr Bikie took a moment to take stock of the old man. He was wearing a scruffy old trench coat and was of unkempt appearance.

He sported a large unruly beard and walked with a distinct limp to one side.

Despite his impairment, the old man started to climb up the ladder towards the stranded Mr Bikie. He passed the point where Mr Bikie was hanging and, taking a length of rope from his pocket, he secured the top of the ladder to the very top of the tree. Then he climbed back down to a point level with Mr Bikie. His breathing had become laboured.

"Give me your hand laddie," said the old man, stretching his own hand out.

The old man managed to grab hold of Mr Bikie's wrist and he pulled him towards the ladder; guiding his hand towards one of the rungs.

"Right laddie," said the old man, "in your own time release your safety buckle and grab hold of my other hand, I'll hold you as best I can."

Mr Bikie looked down at the ground far below. "I'm not sure if that's a good idea," he said. "I don't want to take you down with me if I fall."

"Right you are laddie. You may have a point there. If you're sure that's the way you want it!"

And with that, the old man headed off back down the ladder, leaving Mr Bikie to his own devices.

Mr Bikie was an accomplished mountaineer and once he was certain that the old man was clear, he released the harness that bound him. With cat-like agility he swung his body round to the front of the ladder and planted his feet squarely on to one of its rungs. Then he climbed up and untied the rope that the old man had secured to the top of the tree, before making his way back down to the forest floor.

"Thank you," said Mr Bikie, shaking the old man's hand gratefully, "Malcolm James Bikie is my name or just MJ to my friends."

"Pleasure to meet you MJ," said the old man. "My name is McTavish, Hamish McTavish. People around these parts just know me as McTavish."

The old man looked at Mr Bikie squarely.

"I guess you're not my angel after all then," he said, with deep disappointment in his voice.

"What do you mean, angel?" asked Mr Bikie, "And what did you mean earlier, when you said you had been expecting me?"

"Well," explained the old man, "I had just been praying for help when suddenly you appear. Dropped out of the sky like an angel! I mean it can't be a coincidence, can it? You will help me won't you?"

"Help you?" said Mr Bikie looking puzzled, "But how can I possibly help you?"

"Well laddie, to start with, you can give me a hand to put this ladder back where it belongs."

"Right," said Mr Bikie, looking down into the hole that McTavish had appeared from. "I assume you mean down there?"

"That's right laddie but there's just one thing before we go down there."

"What's that?" asked Mr Bikie.

"You're to tell no one about anything that you might see down there!"

Then he took on a more menacing tone. "Do you understand me, laddie?!"

"Mums the word," said Mr Bikie, a bit too flippantly.

The old man's eyes narrowed towards him!

CHAPTER 7

MCTAVISH'S CAVE

Mr Bikie lowered himself down into the hole and to his surprise found himself in a wide rocky tunnel. An old fashioned oil lantern hanging from a hook on the wall cast barely enough light to illuminate the passageway ahead. McTavish fed the ladder down to him before following it down himself. He took hold of the lantern and gave Mr Bikie a nod to continue down the dark murky tunnel. Mr Bikie, although grateful to McTavish for rescuing him was beginning to wonder where was this old man was taking him with this ladder. As he moved forward he noticed that the tunnel was sloping downwards steeply. They were going deeper and deeper underground. He was starting to feel uneasy about this whole thing!

Suddenly, without warning the ladder he was carrying crashed to the ground behind him and he was plunged into complete darkness. He peered back down the tunnel trying desperately to see where the old man was. His heart pounded in his chest as he called out through the dark.

"McTavish," he called.

He could hear the fear in his voice as it echoed eerily off the tunnel walls.

"McTavish, are you there?"

A dazzling flash of light forced him to shade his eyes momentarily. McTavish was kneeling on the tunnel floor with a match in his hand.

"Sorry about that laddie," he said holding the match to his lantern. "Dammed thing went out. Hope it didn't give you too much of a fright?"

"Perhaps we should swap places," said Mr Bikie, "and you can lead the way!"

"Right you are laddie, most inconsiderate of me. It can be really dangerous down here you know, especially for strangers!" He laughed oddly. "But come to think of it, there haven't been any strangers down here for a very long time." He laughed again adding to Mr Bikie's feeling of unease.

They swapped places and continued their downward path, taking them even deeper underground.

"We'll be coming to a stone staircase soon," called back McTavish. "Wait at the top of the stairs until I get the light sorted out down below. I'll leave my lantern on the hook at the top of the staircase for you. We wouldn't want you accidentally falling down now would we?"

Mr Bikie reached the top of the stone staircase and put his end of the ladder down. To his left was a solid rock wall, but to his right the staircase seemed to drop away to nothing. He watched as McTavish disappeared into the darkness, dragging the ladder behind him. It clattered down one step at a time, and then there was silence.

Taking the lantern from its hook, Mr Bikie raised it high above his head, straining to see what the old man was doing below. A match flared and he watched as McTavish lit an old oil lantern that sat on a large wooden table far below. McTavish blew out the match and discarded it in a tarnished brass ashtray sitting in the centre of the table.

From the top of the staircase, Mr Bikie realised that he was in some sort of vast cavern. It was sparsely furnished with a large wooden table, two sturdy wooden chairs and a metal cabinet sitting against one wall. "Come on down laddie," beckoned McTavish, "come, come and take a seat."

Mr Bikie started down the staircase, taking in his new surroundings as he went. Above him, rising to a height of some sixty feet was a dome-shaped roof. Around the cavern, a number of murals and pictographs had been etched on to the stone walls. At the far end of the cavern, the floor seemed to drop away suddenly, leaving nothing but a black empty space in its place. As Mr Bikie neared the bottom of the staircase McTavish gestured to him yet again.

"Come laddie, come and have a seat. We have things to discuss."

Mr Bikie walked down the last few steps and crossed over to where McTavish was seated. He laid his lantern on top of the table and sat down on the sturdy wooden chair opposite him. McTavish reached into a drawer under the table and produced a tin of rolling tobacco. He proceeded to roll himself a cigarette before lighting it on the naked flame of the oil lantern.

"My apologies," said McTavish. "Where are my manners?" He pushed the tin of tobacco across the table towards Mr Bikie. "I'm not used to guests you see. In fact your are the only other living soul that has ever set eyes on this place."

Only living soul, thought Mr Bikie to himself as he politely pushed the tobacco tin back across the table. Only living soul. What did that mean? There were two chairs at the table. Who had last sat on this very chair in the past, and what had become of them. He did not trust this strange dishevelled old man.

"What is this place?" questioned Mr Bikie.

"This," replied McTavish, somewhat melodramatically, "is the place of my ancestors."

"Your ancestors?" queried Mr Bikie.

"Yes," continued McTavish. "This is the temple of my ancestors, dedicated to the great creatures that once roamed this land and to the beasts that still live around here in the deep." Mr Bikie looked across the table at the old man and decided that he was completely mad.

"And yes," continued McTavish unabated, "most especially this place is dedicated to the Loch Ness Monster herself."

Mr Bikie regarded McTavish with incredulity. "The Loch Ness Monster," he said, repeating the words as though he were in a dream.

"Yes that's right laddie, the Loch Ness Monster," asserted McTavish. "Take a look around you if you don't believe me. I think you will find the drawings on these walls extremely enlightening."

McTavish stood up and thrust one of the oil lanterns across the table to Mr Bikie, gesturing for him to take a look around. Then he resumed his seat and started to roll himself another cigarette. Mr Bikie took hold of the lantern and raised it to shoulder height before setting off around the cavern walls. "Oh! Just one thing laddie," called McTavish after him. He pointed towards the far end of the cavern where the floor dropped away. "Watch yourself down that end laddie. It's dangerous down there!"

Mr Bikie walked over to the nearest wall which was adorned with ancient drawings of prehistoric men hunting with spears and bows. He moved around the wall, and as he did so the drawings became more vivid and more disturbing. There were scenes of ceremonies. Ceremonies, as McTavish had implied, dedicated to the creatures of the deep and to one creature in particular - a creature

41

rising out from the water and devouring sacrifices offered to it. The ceremonies seemed to be taking place in a vast bell-shaped cavern, not dissimilar to the one he now found himself in but on a much greater scale. A large sacrificial stone altar stood beside a vast underground lake. People dressed like ancient priests and priestesses were worshipping and paying homage to the terrifying looking creature.

As he neared the point where the floor dropped away he lowered his lantern and edged forward to get a better look. He could see now that it was a very deep and dark pit. He lowered his lantern further trying to make out what might be down there in that impenetrable darkness. As he leaned over the edge he did not hear McTavish moving up behind him!

CHAPTER 8

TIME TO EXPLORE

"Where's dad?" asked Sprocket as he entered the galley, rubbing the tiredness from his eyes.

"Oh he left hours ago dear," replied Mrs Bikie cracking an egg into the frying pan. "I'm surprised you didn't hear him leave. That boat the gamekeeper arrived in this morning was noisy enough to wake the dead!"

"Oh I forgot about that," said Sprocket taking a seat at the table. "He's gone hang gliding today hasn't he?"

"Yes," replied Mrs Bikie cracking another egg into the pan, "I saw him fly over in his glider earlier this morning. He circled over the hillside a bit then headed off down the loch."

"Oh drat," said Sprocket disappointedly, "I'd liked to have seen that."

"Well you never know dear, he may come back over this way later." She reached into the cupboard and took out some plates. "Do me a big favour and wake up your sister for me will you. Breakfast will be ready soon. Oh and don't forget to wash your hands before breakfast," she added firmly.

Sprocket slouched off to wake up Spindle. Why did his mother keep insisting that he had to wash his hands almost every time she saw him?

43

Five minutes later they were all tucking into a hearty breakfast of bacon and eggs. Spindle slipped Scottie a rasher of bacon under the table when her mother wasn't looking and he wolfed it down hungrily. "Let's go exploring," said Sprocket, buttering himself another piece of toast.

"Not today," said Spindle, "we're going to build our base camp on the beach today, aren't we mummy?"

"Yes dear," replied Mrs Bikie, "we are. But you'll be able to do some exploring later if you want to. That is provided, of course, that you don't wander off too far." She looked at Sprocket pointedly.

Soon the dishes were washed and piled up high on the drying rack. Sprocket went up on deck and started to load the small rubber dinghy that would carry them the short distance to the shore. The others joined him and they all climbed aboard. Scottie planted two paws on the front of the dinghy while Sprocket and Spindle took one oar each. Mrs Bikie sat back and enjoyed the sunshine as she was rowed towards the sandy beach.

Once ashore Spindle helped her mother to gather some twigs and fallen branches while Sprocket found some stones and laid them in a tight circle. They soon had a lively campfire blazing away on the beach. Sprocket assembled his fishing rod and line before finding a good vantage point on a rock beside the shore. He cast his line out into the water and Scottie settled down beside him contentedly. His mother had promised that if he could catch a fish, she would cook it on the campfire for their lunch.

Spindle ran down to the loch's edge with her tadpole net and paddled away happily in the shallow water of the cove. She caught tiny fish which she threw back in and watched as they swam away. Mrs Bikie settled back on a beach towel bathing in the sunshine.

After an hour Sprocket had not caught a single fish and Spindle was getting bored. "Let's go exploring," she shouted across to Sprocket, who was staring intently at the float some twenty metres off shore.

Sprocket, although desperately wanting to catch a fish, was getting a bit fed up with his lack of success. He pulled in the fishing line and along with Spindle and Scottie, they went back to where Mrs Bikie was basking herself in the sun. "I'm bored," said Sprocket to his mother. "Can we go exploring now? Please!"

Mrs Bikie sat up, shading her eyes from the glare of the sun as she looked up at the children. "But you haven't caught any fish yet," she said.

"Oh I'm fed up with fishing," said Sprocket. "I haven't even had as much as a nibble. Why don't you give it a try for me mum? I'll show you how, and you can carry on fishing while we go exploring."

Mrs Bikie considered the offer; she wouldn't mind trying her hand at catching a fish.

"OK then," she said, "but remember what I told you about not going too far and don't be away for too long either!"

"We won't," Sprocket assured her.

Mrs Bikie followed the children down to the water's edge where Sprocket had left his rod and line. Then the children set off to explore, leaving Mrs Bikie content to try her luck at fishing.

"Let's follow the shoreline down the loch," said Sprocket. "Mum said that she saw dad flying in that direction earlier this morning. We might be lucky enough to spot him!"

"OK," said Spindle, skipping along beside him happily.

They carried on down the shoreline, throwing pebbles into the loch as they went. The beach started to narrow and eventually it petered out to a point where a sheer cliff stretched down into the waters of the loch. "It's a dead-end," said Spindle. "We'd better go back." She turned to head back, but Sprocket had other ideas.

"No, look, there's a path that runs up the side of the cliff. I bet it goes over the top and on to another beach."

Spindle looked at the path not wishing to go any further. "It looks dangerous to me," she said, "and anyway, mum said we were not to go too far!"

"Oh don't be such a scaredy-cat," said Sprocket dismissively. "If it gets too difficult we'll turn back okay?" Without waiting for a reply he set off up the path with Scottie, leaving Spindle little choice but to follow on reluctantly.

The path, very steep and narrow at first, soon started to level out and widen. At one point they could see a waterfall in the distance cascading down a mountain before mysteriously disappearing into what looked like solid rock. The path narrowed again then dropped down steeply into a wooded area. Spindle continued to follow Sprocket, afraid now to be without her elder brother.

"Look!" exclaimed Sprocket excitedly as they emerged from the trees. "Look down there. There's a big building of some sort. It looks like... it looks like a monastery!"

"Let's go back," said Spindle unhappily. "I want to go back to camp now."

"Oh don't be silly. Let's take a closer look," said Sprocket, excited at his new find.

He pressed on, ignoring Spindle's pleas to turn back but stopped when he reached a large notice nailed to a post by the side of the path. Spindle came up beside him and they both looked at the sign.

It read: WARNING. KEEP OUT. And below, in red paint, a skull and crossbones added weight to the message.

"I'm not going any further," said Spindle firmly, her voice indicating that this time she really meant it. "I'm going back."

Sprocket was in two minds, but he tried to persuade Spindle to carry on.

As they argued the point, a dark shadow cast over them blocking out the sunlight. Scottie gave a long low growl and they turned to find themselves dwarfed by a giant cloaked figure. A terrifying looking monk with a deep scar running down one side of his face stood in front of them clothed from head to foot in black. His cold grey eyes fell upon them.

"What are you kids up to?" roared the cloaked figure in a foreign accent. "Can't you read?"

His voice was thunderous, casting fear into the startled children. Sprocket was first to muster up the courage to speak.

"We're looking for our father," he said, his voice trembling. "He was hang gliding this way earlier and we thought we might see him."

"So that was your father," said the monk knowingly, and then in a menacing tone, "What is his name?"

Spindle opened her mouth to speak but Sprocket elbowed her in the ribs. "We're going now," said Sprocket, grabbing Spindle's hand and pulling her after him. They ran back up the path with Scottie hard on their heels.

"If I see you around here again you'll be sorry!" shouted the monk after them.

Sprocket and Spindle ran and ran until their lungs were close to bursting. They soon found themselves back on the beach.

"I'm telling mum about that monk," panted Spindle. She looked back up the path. "Do you think he followed us?"

"No," replied Sprocket, "and you'd better not tell mum or you'll just get us both into trouble."

Spindle blamed Sprocket for leading them astray but she nodded in agreement.

As they ran back along the shoreline towards the *Highland Princess* the black-cloaked monk appeared on the brow of the cliff path, watching them menacingly. He had found the place where those pesky children stayed and even better the location of the hang gliding man who had been snooping around earlier. He would take care of them all. Nobody was going to stand in his way.

A cruel smile crept onto his face as he adjusted his hood and turned back towards the monastery.

CHAPTER 9

DOWN THE PIT

Startled, Mr Bikie swung round and stared straight into McTavish's eyes. McTavish returned his stare searchingly. "What's the matter laddie?" said McTavish. "Did you think I was going to push you over the edge?"

Mr Bikie made no reply.

"You can trust me laddie. Now give me a hand to get this ladder back into place. I want you to see what's down there." He pointed down into the deep dark pit.

They went back to where the ladder was lying on the cavern floor and once again Mr Bikie picked up his end. Under McTavish's direction, the two men worked together to lower the ladder down the pit. McTavish then knotted a short piece of rope to the top rung and tied the other end to a purpose-built spike that had been hammered into the cavern floor.

"We'd better get the safety gear," said McTavish.

McTavish limped over to the metal cupboard situated against the cavern wall and produced two helmets and two powerful torches. He handed one set to Mr Bikie. "Let the tour begin," he said in a light-hearted manner.

With some difficulty McTavish swung his bad leg over the side of the pit. Mr Bikie followed him and they started their slow but steady descent.

On reaching the bottom McTavish greeted Mr Bikie enthusiastically. "Well done laddie!" he said.

Mr Bikie took a few moments to take in his new surroundings. He had expected to find himself in another cave but realised that the pit was no more than a shaft, dropping down to another level. A wide passageway led off in one direction, perhaps towards the loch, he couldn't be sure? McTavish led the way and Mr Bikie followed close behind.

The passageway sloped steeply downwards, and as they descended, the walls became green and slimy as water wept out of them.

"Watch your step here laddie," warned McTavish, "it's treacherously slippery down here."

Mr Bikie needed no telling as he had already slipped a couple of times. He had set out that morning to go hang gliding, not caving. Now, by some freakish twist of fate, he found himself inextricably caught up in some strange new quest. McTavish was taking him to who knows where, but curiosity had got the better of him. He had to know what was at the far end of this tunnel.

McTavish came to a halt as the beam from his torch fell upon a narrow wooden bridge. The bridge spanned a circular hole in the passage floor. Mr Bikie stepped forward and shone his torch down into the abyss, straining to see what lay below. Strange, he thought to himself, this hole appeared to have no walls, and from here it looked bottomless. He could hear the sound of gushing water and as he scoured the vast empty space his torch caught the glint of something far below, perhaps hundreds of feet below. It was a waterfall. A cascading tumbling underground waterfall.

"Where are we?" asked Mr Bikie, turning to McTavish. "What is this place and what's down there?"

"Nessie's Cave," answered McTavish in a mysterious tone. "We're on the very roof of Nessie's Cave."

"How do we get down there?" asked Mr Bikie, feeling a sudden rush of excitement.

"This passageway continues on the far side of this bridge," replied McTavish. "Eventually it will take us down to the water's edge. I think this part of the passageway must have caved in some time ago, or perhaps, it's always been like this, nobody can know for sure."

Mr Bikie shone his torch at the narrow wooden bridge. It was of simple construction, consisting of two tree trunks crudely lashed together with some old rope. Short planks of wood were nailed across its length to make it easier to cross. But over the years, green slime had covered its length, making it extremely treacherous to navigate. It was then that Mr Bikie noticed a climbing ring that had been hammered into the stone floor beside the bridge. He wondered why it had been placed there.

"We'll have to go across on all fours," advised McTavish, "it's far too slippery and dangerous to walk across."

"Come," said McTavish, "I'll go first. Once I'm safely over to the other side you can follow."

McTavish knelt down and slowly edged his way across the bridge. On reaching the other side he turned and beckoned for Mr Bikie to join him. "Come on laddie," he called, "nice and easy now."

Mr Bikie kneeled down onto the slimy surface and cautiously made the perilous crossing. McTavish greeted him warmly on the other side.

"Well done laddie," he said delightedly. "I'm not too keen on that bit myself."

"I'm not surprised," said Mr Bikie, looking back across the bridge.

The passageway dropped steeply now, spiralling downwards, down to Nessie's Cave. As they descended the sound of gushing water grew louder. Finally, they reached the end of the passageway and stepped out into a vast cavern.

"Nessie's Cave," announced McTavish reverently. He reached into his coat pocket and pulled out a small hand-held flare which he lit with a match. Mr Bikie watched as McTavish raised the flare high above his head and walked down to the water's edge. He was muttering something to himself as he went, as though praying, or perhaps, paying homage to something. Somehow it reminded him of the drawings he had seen on the cave wall and of the high priest standing beside an underground lake.

Mr Bikie joined McTavish and they stood together at the edge of the lake, enchanted by the immense beauty surrounding them.

Nessie's Cave was bell-shaped and of cathedral-sized proportions. It stretched upwards into the darkness and to the bridge they had just crossed. Mineral deposits on the walls twinkled and sparkled in the white light of the flare. It was as if the walls were covered with a million glittering jewels. The waterfall was most spellbinding of all. It gushed out from the rock on the far side of the lake, depositing its frothy white foam into the jet black waters.

"It's magnificent," said Mr Bikie in wonderment. "Nessie's Cave. It's incredible... Nessie's Cave," he repeated.

"Not many have ever seen this laddie," commented McTavish. "Not in modern times anyway."

"But why me?" asked Mr Bikie. "Why are you showing me all this now?"

McTavish looked perplexed as though he were trying to resolve some inner conflict. He regarded Mr Bikie and once again his eyes narrowed. Could he really trust this man and tell him everything? But before he could reply their attention was drawn towards something in the water, something arising from the depths below!

"What is that?" asked Mr Bikie uncertainly.

"It's him!" cried McTavish. "Quick, switch off your torch before he sees us!"

McTavish threw his flare onto the stone floor and stamped it out frantically. As instructed, Mr Bikie switched off his torch, plunging them into darkness. But it was not complete darkness; it was a kind of unearthly gloom. As the two men peered down into the depths of the lake they could see what looked like two enormous luminous eyes coming up towards them.

"Run!" screamed McTavish taking flight. "Run for your life!"

But Mr Bikie stayed rooted to the spot, transfixed as the luminous eyes gazed up at him. He held his ground, he had to be certain. Then he knew. It was not the monster. It was the submarine he had seen earlier!

CHAPTER 10

ON THE RUN

The hull of the submarine broke surface nose first and the glare from the two powerful headlights blinded him momentarily. He could just make out a cloaked figure emerging from the submarine's turret. As he took flight, shots rang out, echoing around the cavern walls. He flicked on his torch as he plunged back into the passageway leading up to the bridge and started his steep ascent up the spiralling pathway.

Already he could hear the sound of boots running behind him, gaining on him with every step. Orders were being barked out in some foreign accent, as his murderous and determined pursuers gave chase. The monks were trying to kill him, and he had no idea why?

He would soon reach the bridge; perhaps that would slow them down. Where was McTavish? What had happened to him? As he approached the bridge a hand emerged from the shadows and grabbed hold of him, pulling him backwards forcibly.

"Shh, it's me laddie," said McTavish whispering into his ear. "Switch off your torch, it's this way."

In total darkness, McTavish pulled Mr Bikie into a narrow crack in the passage wall.

"It's a wee bit of a squeeze here laddie," said McTavish keeping his voice to a whisper.

Mr Bikie could feel the sides of the stone walls closing in on him, but even in the pitch black, he sensed that the crack in the wall was starting to widen again. They were entering another cave. He felt McTavish's hand rest on his arm, a signal for him to stop. The approaching voices were getting louder and they stood together in the dark hardly daring to breathe, fearful that they would betray their position. The pursuing party was made up of three men. The leader named Hans spoke first.

"There were two of them," he said. "I'm sure of it. I saw two of them as we surfaced."

"I only saw one," stated one of the other men named Darrius.

"No. There were definitely two of them," Hans insisted.

All three men stopped dead when they reached the narrow bridge.

"You cross over first Darrius," ordered Hans.

"You must be joking," responded Darrius. "I'm not crossing over that bridge for anybody!"

"You'll do as I tell you," said Hans, levelling his gun at him.

"We can get them later," protested Darrius defiantly.

"We shall get them now!" insisted Hans. "Stand aside! I shall cross first and if you know what's good for you, you had better follow me. Otherwise, your contract will be terminated permanently, if you get my meaning."

Hans stepped on to the bridge. He managed no more than a few steps before the treacherous bridge took his feet from under him. He cried out in pain as his left shoulder impacted on the deck of the bridge and his cry turned to a full-blown scream as he plunged headlong off the bridge and into the darkness below. Darrius and the other man froze as the piercing scream ended with a muffled splash.

"Well I guess that countermands that order!" sneered Darrius. He turned to the other man, known as Weasel. "We'd better get back down there and see what's left of him. Von Heinrich wouldn't like it if anything has happened to his precious right-hand man."

"Who cares if he lives or dies," snarled Weasel. "One less to share with, that's what I say."

"I don't know if Von Heinrich will see it that way when we get back to the monastery," said Darrius. "Come on, we'd better get down there and pick up the pieces."

Mr Bikie and McTavish listened from their hiding place as Darrius and Weasel made their way back down the path. McTavish, satisfied that they were gone, turned on his torch.

"We'll be safe now," said McTavish. "If they come back this way they'll not be able to find this passageway easily."

"Passageway – passageway to where?"

"To the castle!" replied McTavish. "This way laddie."

"Wait!" exclaimed Mr Bikie. "Before I go any further I want to know what's going on around here! Why were those men trying to kill us?"

McTavish turned to face Mr Bikie, and once again his eyes narrowed towards him. He had already shown Mr Bikie more than any other living soul. Could he trust this stranger with his secret? He felt as though he no longer had a choice.

"Very well," said McTavish, "I'll tell you, but not here, not now. And before I tell you anything, you have to make me a promise."

"A promise?" queried Mr Bikie, "what sort of promise?"

"I have a secret," said McTavish. "I want you to promise that if I tell you what is happening around here you will keep it to yourself. That you will never reveal it to another living soul."

"I don't know if I can agree to that," responded Mr Bikie. "I don't know what you're getting me involved in here."

"Promise! Or you'll know nothing!" shouted McTavish, raising his voice and stepping towards him.

"Very well then, I promise!" shouted back Mr Bikie, the words tumbling out of his mouth before he had time to stop them.

McTavish hesitated for a moment, and then he smiled. He raised his arm and cheerfully patted Mr Bikie on the shoulder.

"Thank you laddie," he said. "A burden shared is a burden halved! I'll tell you everything once we get out of this place."

Mr Bikie began to reflect on what had just happened. What was it he was getting himself involved in? What, exactly, had he foolishly just agreed to?

The cave they were in narrowed into a passageway which rose steeply until finally, it came to an abrupt end at a solid stone wall.

"Hold my torch for me laddie," said McTavish.

Mr Bikie took hold of the torch and directed its beam onto the stone wall. In the centre, a metal ring had been attached. McTavish took hold of the ring and pulled it with all his might. Slowly at first, then gathering pace, the wall started to swing open. As it did so Mr Bikie shone the torch through the narrow gap into what looked like a small underground chamber.

"After you laddie," gestured McTavish.

They passed through the newly made opening and McTavish pulled the wall closed using a metal ring that had been set into the far side. Mr Bikie surveyed his dark and dismal surroundings.

"What is this place?" asked Mr Bikie.

"We're in the dungeons of the castle," replied McTavish. "These walls have witnessed terrible things laddie. Many unfortunate souls had suffered imprisonment, torture and death at the hands of their captors here. Some may even have been taken through that wall and sacrificed on the altar to the creature.

Mr Bikie turned his attention to the heavy wooden door that was set into the far wall of the cell. He walked over and tried to open it. "We appear to be locked in!" he said turning to McTavish.

"Don't worry laddie," said McTavish, taking a rusty old set of keys from his coat pocket. He jingled them in the air mischievously. "I have a copy of every key in this castle."

They journeyed up through the dungeons and McTavish unlocked every door and gate that came in their way. Finally, they climbed the last flight of stairs and burst out into brilliant sunshine in the castle grounds.

As they walked hurriedly across the lawns towards the exit, a small boy was watching them from far above on the castle battlements. "Look mummy!" he exclaimed. "It's that flying man and he's escaping from the dungeons with his friend."

Wee Johnny's mother looked down at Mr Bikie and McTavish. They did have the appearance of two men trying to escape from something, but she dismissed Wee Johnny's observation out of hand.

"Don't be silly Johnny," said his mother. "There haven't been any prisoners kept in those dungeons for hundreds of years. Now it's time for us to go for our lunch. I've paid full board at that hotel and I'm not going to miss out on my lunch for anything. If you're a good boy we'll come back here tomorrow and explore the rest of the castle."

Mr Bikie and McTavish headed up the steep path that led to the exit. They came to a stop when they reached the castle car park. Mr Bikie turned to McTavish.

"Well? You said you were going to tell me everything. What exactly is going on around here?" he demanded.

"I will tell you!" said McTavish. "I'll meet you tonight and tell you everything."

"Where?" asked Mr Bikie.

"At the Castle Hotel in the village," replied McTavish. "That's where I work. I should be finished around eight o'clock. Meet me in the beer garden at the back of the hotel. I'll tell you everything then!"

Mr Bikie watched as McTavish limped off in the direction of the village, his mind reeling with the day's events.

What would McTavish tell him that evening? Why were those monks trying to kill them and what exactly was McTavish's secret?

CHAPTER 11

THE BIKE SHOP

Mr Bikie crossed over the castle car park and jumped onto the first bus bound for Inverness. From there he caught a connecting service to Aviemore. As the fields whizzed past his window he closed his eyes and drifted off to sleep. It seemed like an age ago since only that morning he had launched himself and his hang glider off the summit Carn Gorm. It was late afternoon before the bus finally came to a stop outside Aviemore Railway Station, jolting him out of his sleep. As he got off the bus he was greeted by his old friend Stuart Campbell.

"Ah, you're here at last," said Stuart, "I've been expecting you!"

Not again, thought Mr Bikie, everybody seemed to be expecting him nowadays.

"Why would you be expecting me?" he asked his friend.

"Did you not get my text message then?"

"No," replied Mr Bikie "my mobile has been down for the past few days, what was it about?"

"Oh," said Stuart frowning. "Well, you know you asked me to keep an eye on your shop for you while you were away."

"Yes," replied Mr Bikie, hardly daring to imagine what might come next.

"Well, I passed by your shop this morning and there was a whole fleet of delivery vans outside, unloading boxes and boxes of stuff. I thought I'd better text you and let you know about it, you know what Mr Bumble is like."

Oh heavens, thought Mr Bikie to himself. What had his hapless shop assistant, Mr Bumble, managed to do in the few short days he had been away?"

"I'd better get along there right away. Thanks for letting me know Stuart. See you later."

"Oh and there's something else," called Stuart after him. "PC Lockum's been looking for you, something to do with a boat accident up in Inverness?"

PC Lockum was new to the village, having been transferred there from another area. It was fair to say that he had become a bit of a thorn in Mr Bikie's side. It all started when a number of bicycles were stolen locally. PC Lockum was convinced that Mr Bikie was the mastermind behind this crime spree, and ever since had been keeping a close eye on him.

He thanked Stuart again and made his way hurriedly along the main street towards his bicycle shop. As he entered the shop his worst fears were realised. Stacked to the ceiling, taking up every available inch of space were small brown cardboard boxes, thousands of them. A narrow walkway between the boxes led through from the front shop to the serving counter at the rear. Two men squeezed passed him on their way out.

"I thought you said this place sold bicycles," he heard one of them say.

"Well it did the other day," replied his friend. "They had one of the finest bike displays I've ever seen!"

Mr Bikie approached the counter. Sitting behind it on a high chair was his hapless shop assistant Mr Bumble, busily examining some paperwork in front of him. He looked up in surprise when he saw Mr Bikie.

"Oh! Mr Bikie!" he exclaimed, pushing the papers to one side. "I wasn't expecting you. I thought you were on holiday?"

"I was," replied Mr Bikie dryly.

"Well, it's been really busy around here since you left," confided Mr Bumble, "and as you can see, that order you asked me to place arrived this morning. Marvellous isn't it? To think I only ordered it yesterday and here it is. I must write a letter to the suppliers on your behalf congratulating them on such an excellent service."

"What order? I didn't ask you to order all this!" said Mr Bikie waving his arms around in the air angrily.

"The right-hand brake handles," said Mr Bumble. "The ones you asked me to order on your behalf." He gestured towards the boxes, smiling with the satisfaction at a job well done.

"I wanted you to order nine right-hand brake handles. Not thousands of them!" said Mr Bikie, looking around at all the boxes towering above him.

Mr Bumble frowned and started to shuffle about some bits of paper on the counter. "Ah here we are. In your very own handwriting," he added triumphantly. "Nine thousand, four hundred and thirty-one, right-hand brake handles." He handed the piece of paper over to Mr Bikie for him to examine. It read - Bike Handles (right) 9-431

"This says nine," said Mr Bikie irritably. "The other three figures are the catalogue number, which in this case is 431."

"Oh dear," said Mr Bumble, "an easy mistake to make, wouldn't you say Mr Bikie?"

Before Mr Bikie could reply a customer entered the shop and approached the counter. He looked puzzled as he surveyed the piles   and   piles   of   boxes   around him.

"Excuse me," he asked politely. "Is this by any chance the village bike shop?"

"It certainly is," beamed Mr Bumble. "How can I help you?"

"I don't suppose you happen to have any right-hand brake handles do you?"

Mr Bumble looked delighted.

"It's your lucky day," said Mr Bumble enthusiastically. "They just came into stock this morning. Now how many would you like? We have a good stock of them!"

"Oh, just the one please," replied the customer, "and do you by any chance have anyone who would be able to fit it?

"We certainly do," beamed Mr Bumble getting up from his chair. "It's a bit crowded in here at the moment, so if it's okay with you I'll fit it for you outside."

He edged his way around the counter and squeezed past Mr Bikie.

"You see," said Mr Bumble, "they're selling like hot cakes. Pile them high and sell them cheap. That's what I say! Oh, and before I forget, PC Lockum was in here looking for you, something about taking a statement. He's been acting very strangely since that business with the stolen bicycles. He wanted to know what you were doing up there in Inverness. I told him you were on holiday. He said he was off-duty for the rest of the week and would catch up with you when he gets back."

Mr Bumble hurried out of the shop to fit the customers brake handle, leaving Mr Bikie to look around in dismay at all the cardboard boxes. He reached for the phone and called the supplier. After he had given the supplier several apologies for the mix-up, the lady at the other end of the phone saw the funny side and agreed to take the bike handles back for a small administration fee. This, considered Mr Bikie, was better than being stuck with thousands of right-hand brake handles. It would take him a lifetime to sell that many.

He wrote a short note to Mr Bumble explaining what he had done and asking him not to put in any more orders until he came back from holiday. Mr Bumble would find the note and wonder where he had disappeared to, but after a short while, he would forget all about it and not give it another thought. For Mr Bikie's purposes, Mr Bumble was the perfect assistant.

He made his way into the back shop and started to move piles of cardboard boxes that had been stacked up high in front of a large, double-doored stationary cabinet. He took a set of keys from his pocket and unlocked the cabinet doors before stepping in and locking the doors behind him. There was a swishing sound as the back panel of the cabinet slid open to reveal a long well-lit corridor. He walked briskly down the corridor. Another panel door opened in front of him and he entered his secret warehouse that had been built into the hillside behind his shop. He passed shelf after shelf of equipment, but for now all he wanted was his bike and the crystal.

From one of the shelves he took down a small ornate hand-carved wooden box. He had seen the contents of the box many times before, but its beauty never failed to impress him. Cradled inside the silk-lined box was a small egg-shaped golden casket, studded with precious gems. He lifted the delicate silver catch and as he did so a mysterious ringing sound resonated as the crystal inside energised. A brilliant spectrum of light cast out in all directions.

He took the crystal to his bike, which was still leaning against his highly polished desk and unscrewed the top of the bicycle bell. Taking great care he set the crystal inside and replaced the top. The same mysterious sound now emanated from his bike. He straddled the bike and placed his palm over the top of the bell. There was a blinding flash and he was gone.

CHAPTER 12

THE CASTLE HOTEL

The Castle Hotel was a baronial mansion that had long ago been converted into a hotel. Its grandeur had diminished over the years leaving it shabby and run down in appearance.

Mr Bikie shackled his bike to the rack next to the hotel's entrance and unclipped the bell from its handlebars. He tucked the bell safely away in his pocket before making his way up the impressive granite staircase to the main door.

The hallway, despite the threadbare carpet, remained impressively grand. The reception desk at the far end of the hall was unattended so he followed the signs for the public bar. Eventually he entered a large high ceilinged room which had been converted into a bistro.

He ordered a drink at the bar and asked the barmaid for directions to the beer garden. She pointed to a set of double doors and he thanked her before making his way outside. A glance at his watch told him that he was early. It was only seven-thirty, plenty of time before he had to meet up with McTavish. He settled down and took a sip of his beer. As he laid his glass back down on the table a small boy entered the beer garden and walked straight towards him.

"Excuse me sir. Pardon me for asking, but aren't you the flying man who was at the castle earlier this morning?"

Mr Bikie looked up in surprise. He recognised the small boy as the one he had seen with his mother on the battlements just before he had crashed his glider.

"Yes," replied Mr Bikie, "I suppose I am."

"My name is Johnny," continued the small boy, offering Mr Bikie his hand in a very grown-up manner. "Everybody calls me Wee Johnny," he added matter-of-factly.

"Pleasure to meet you Wee Johnny," said Mr Bikie, taking his small outstretched hand and shaking it warmly.

"My name is Malcolm James Bikie. But please call me MJ."

"I saw you later on as well in the castle grounds. You were trying to escape from something, weren't you?"

Mr Bikie looked at Wee Johnny in astonishment.

"How did you know that?" he asked.

"I just know!" said Wee Johnny. "Sometimes I feel a bit like escaping myself. I'm going to be an explorer when I grow up!"

Before Mr Bikie could reply, the voice of a woman rang out shrilly from the main building. "Johnny. Wee Johnny, where are you?"

"I have to go now!" said Wee Johnny looking back towards the double-doors.

Wee Johnny's mother entered the beer garden. "Ah, there you are! Haven't I told you about wandering off on your own like that?"

She walked over to where Mr Bikie was sitting and grabbed Wee Johnny by the hand before glaring down at Mr Bikie angrily. Wee Johnny turned and waved goodbye as his mother dragged him off after her.

Eight o'clock came and went. Ten past eight. Twenty past eight and there was still no sign of McTavish. By half-past eight, Mr Bikie had finished his beer and decided another was in order. The barmaid was no longer on duty and her place had been taken by a portly man, who judging by his appearance was the hotel manager.

"Pint sir?" asked the manager.

"Yes please," responded Mr Bikie rummaging around in his pocket for some change.

As the manager pulled him a pint, he decided to ask after McTavish. "Do you by any chance know a Mr McTavish? He told me he works here at the hotel."

The manager eyed Mr Bikie suspiciously, making no immediate reply.

"He does work here doesn't he?" prompted Mr Bikie.

The manager grunted. "If you can call it work," he snorted. "He washes the pots and pans in the kitchen, but I could train a monkey to do a better job. This is a busy time of year sir. He'll be out of the kitchen when he's good and finished, and not a moment sooner."

Mr Bikie took an instant dislike to the manager and especially his lowly appraisal of McTavish.

"Perhaps you would be good enough to tell him I'm here," said Mr Bikie, paying for his drink. "Please tell him that I'm waiting for him in the beer garden."

The manager eyed Mr Bikie's back as he walked away from the bar, curious as to what this stranger might want with McTavish. Mr Bikie was about to pass through the double doors leading into the beer garden when he turned and made his way back to the bar. He addressed the manager once again. "Do you have a bag of crisps please?" he asked, dipping into his pocket for some small change.

The manager reached under the counter and produced a packet of crisps. "Here we go sir."

"Tell me," said Mr Bikie, accepting the crisps, though not really wanting them, "have you known Mr McTavish for long?"

"Long enough," replied the manager. "He's lived in these parts all his life as far as I know. Since his accident he hasn't been quite right in the head, a bit touched you know."

The manager made a circular motion around the side of his ear with his forefinger to emphasise the point.

"Accident?" asked Mr Bikie.

"Yes," said the manager, "a diving accident he says. That's when he says he snagged his leg and was crippled. Anyway since McTavish had his accident he has been working here, let me see now, that would be about six years now. I only keep him on out of the goodness of my heart." He puffed his chest out with self-importance. "This place is up for sale at the moment sir. And I can promise you that when the new owners take over, he'll be out on his ear. They won't be keeping him on. Well not if they've got any sense they won't."

"What do you mean by him being a bit touched?" asked Mr Bikie.

"Well…" said the manager warming to the conversation. He leaned forward with a hushed voice. "He tells stories doesn't he! The old fool claims that it was the Loch Ness Monster that shattered his leg. Folks around here say that his family have spent three generations looking for the monster!" the manager sniggered dismissively. "After a few drinks he'll tell you the same thing sir - you see if he doesn't. He tells that story to tourists so that he can cadge a few drinks off them. Don't you pay no attention to him sir or he'll con you out of a few drinks as well!"

The manager, having given up all this information, was about to ask Mr Bikie what his business was with McTavish. But Mr Bikie, anticipating his question, thanked him for the crisps and turned abruptly to make his way back to the beer garden.

One of the waitresses entered the beer garden and started to collect empty glasses from the tables. She reached Mr Bikie's table.

"Can I get you anything to eat sir?" she asked politely.

"No, I'm fine thank you," replied Mr Bikie, gesturing to his bag of crisps. "I'm just waiting for someone."

"You're waiting for McTavish, aren't you sir?

"Yes," replied Mr Bikie, "do you know him?"

"He's in the kitchen at the moment sir, but the boss won't let him finish his shift. He knows you're waiting for him sir and he sends his apologies."

"Do you know how much longer he'll be?"

"I'm afraid not sir, but I think he'll be some time yet. The manager's got it in for him, if you know what I mean sir. It's terrible the way that man treats him, like a piece of dirt. I dare say he won't even pay McTavish for his overtime!" She picked up an empty glass from the next table and clattered it down on to her tray in an agitated manner before continuing.

"He was a proud man once sir, a great diver. That was before his accident. Well I've said enough sir. I'd better get back to work. Just remember this," she said before departing. "He's a good man is McTavish. McTavish is a good man!"

"Wait!" called Mr Bikie after her. "What is your name?"

"Beth sir. My name is Beth." And with that she left the beer garden, leaving Mr Bikie to ponder her words.

McTavish finally arrived in the beer garden at the back of nine o'clock. He could not apologise enough for being so late. Mr Bikie ordered him a beer.

"Now," said Mr Bikie. "I think it's time you tell me what's going on around here. Why were those men shooting at us this morning?"

McTavish took a mouthful of his beer and leaned back into his chair. "Well," he said, clearing his throat, "it all started over a hundred years ago, just as the First World War was coming to an end."

CHAPTER 13

MCTAVISH'S SECRET

"It began on the 6th of November 1918. A young naval officer of the German High Seas Fleet named Baron Von Heinrich was serving on the battleship SMS Kronprinz Wilhelm.

"The First World War was coming to an end and there was unrest in the rank and file of the German Fleet. Some crews had even mutinied. The SMS Kronprinz Wilhelm had been ordered to sail from the German port of Kiel to a secret rendezvous point somewhere off the coast of Sweden. There were only two men on board who knew their final destination and nature of their mission, the ship's Captain and the Communications Officer, Baron Von Heinrich. Baron Von Heinrich was no ordinary crew member though; he was an aristocrat and an internationally acclaimed mountaineer with close ties to royalty.

"The captain took his orders directly from the Kaiser himself. The Kaiser, knowing that Germany would be thrown into political unrest after the war, made arrangements for his vast wealth of gold and precious jewels to be assembled, ready for transportation overseas. The most precious part of his fabulous wealth was loaded aboard the SMS Kronprinz Wilhelm which set sail the following day. The Kaiser had calculated that there was still time for the ship to complete its mission before an armistice between Germany and the Allies was signed. But, unfortunately for him, the ship was delayed when it developed engine trouble at sea.

"On November 11 1918, the armistice was signed and the German High Seas Fleet were ordered to divert to the Orkney Islands in Scotland. The Captain of the SMS Kronprinz Wilhelm had no option but to comply with the terms of the armistice or risk causing his countrymen further unnecessary bloodshed.

"The Royal Navy escorted the German High Seas Fleet to the natural harbour of Scapa Flow in the Orkney Islands; there to be interned. Many of the sailors were allowed to return to Germany, but skeleton crews were left aboard.

"The ship's Captain along with Baron Von Heinrich stayed with their ship, planning all the while for their precious cargo to be smuggled out of Scapa Flow and transported to Sweden as originally ordered. However, before their plan could be actioned, on 21 June 1919, Admiral Von Reuter gave orders for the German Fleet to be scuttled. The Captain of the SMS Kronprinz Wilhelm complied with these orders before he and his skeleton crew took to the lifeboats.

"During their attempt to abandon the sinking ship and the ensuing confusion, some of the British forces guarding them opened fire. The Captain was fatally wounded, leaving Baron Von Heinrich the only man alive who knew of the existence of the treasure that had gone down with his ship. Baron Von Heinrich was made a prisoner of war and then later repatriated to his native Germany."

McTavish paused and took a long drink from his glass before continuing.

"On his return, he noticed enormous changes had taken place in his homeland and that the Kaiser had been deposed. Von Heinrich decided he no longer held any allegiance to his former masters, and so he made his plans to recover the fabulous treasure for himself. Some years passed. Then in the summer of 1923, he returned to the Orkney Islands and rented a cottage at Lyness on the shores of Scapa Flow.

"Von Heinrich was an accomplished mountaineer but he was no diver. It was then that he met my great-grandfather and they struck up a friendship. Von Heinrich enlisted my great-grandfather's help to recover the lost treasure. My great-grandfather taught Von Heinrich how to dive and how to work the surface equipment. After a few months of intensive training, they were ready to make their first attempt to recover the treasure.

"There was still a heavy naval presence in the bay and they were afraid of being discovered. So the two men set out in the dead of night in a rowing boat. Good fortune was on their side and they were successful. Baron Von Heinrich and my great-grandfather returned to the cottage with the treasure, there to decide what to do next.

"They realised that it would be difficult to dispose of all that treasure on the international markets without arousing suspicion. So they decided to store the treasure in a safe place and sell it off bit by bit. That's when my great-grandfather told Baron Von Heinrich about the secret that had been passed down through generations of my family, the existence of Nessie's Cave.

"From the Orkney Islands they crossed over to the mainland before transporting the treasure by road, here to Drumnadrochit. Both men then mysteriously disappeared, never to be seen again!"

McTavish took another drink from his glass and waited for Mr

Bikie's response. Mr Bikie leaned forward in his chair.

"That's quite a story! You say that your great-grandfather's friend was called Von Heinrich? Isn't that the name we overheard one of those men say when they were chasing us in Nessie's Cave? He said Hans was Von Heinrich's 'precious right-hand man'."

"That's right laddie, and he's back here to claim the treasure."

"Back here," said Mr Bikie. "But that's impossible. If he were still alive now, he would be well over a hundred years old!"

"Oh, he's alive all right," said McTavish, "and what's more I've seen him recently. Right here in Drumnadrochit! He didn't see me of course but I saw him all right. And I'm telling you he doesn't look a day older than he did in 1923."

McTavish took an old photograph from his pocket and slipped it across the table. "That's him, Baron Von Heinrich with my great-grandfather taken in 1923."

"But it can't be the same Von Heinrich. It's just not possible," contended Mr Bikie.

"I can only tell you what I saw," contested McTavish. "You heard what those men said - 'Von Heinrich'. Look at that picture, those lean spidery features, cruel hawkish eyes and that scar down his right cheek. He stands over six feet six inches tall; he's not an easy man to mistake. It couldn't be anyone else."

"Perhaps he is a relative of his," suggested Mr Bikie, "one of his descendants perhaps?" It might be that one of his descendants has somehow found out about the existence of the treasure and has come here in search of it?"

McTavish looked thoughtful. "Yes, it's a possibility I suppose. I hadn't really considered that."

"The monastery," said Mr Bikie. "The one on the other side of the loch. Do you know it?"

"The monastery - yes, why do you ask?"

"Because I think that is where Von Heinrich and his gang are hanging out. I saw them over there this morning heading down the path towards the boathouse. Those men that took a pot-shot at us this afternoon were also dressed as monks. I saw one of them as the submarine emerged from the lake."

The two men fell silent for a moment, digesting what had been said. Mr Bikie broke the silence first.

"How long have you been looking for the treasure?" he enquired.

"All my life," replied McTavish. "I've spent my entire lifetime searching for that treasure."

McTavish's voice became emotional.

"After my accident, I just gave up. It's not that I can't dive any more — maybe I could if I tried. It's just that… it's just that I'm afraid!" He paused for a moment. "That's why I was praying for an angel to help me. That's when you arrived."

"Afraid?" asked Mr Bikie, "Afraid of what?"

"Of the monster of course," said McTavish, looking Mr Bikie straight in the eye. "The Loch Ness Monster!"

Mr Bikie said nothing as McTavish continued.

"It was the monster that did this to me," said McTavish, banging his clenched fist against his crippled leg. "I was down there diving in the cave near the place where it opens out into the loch. It was then that the creature got hold of me. It was horrible, terrifying. It had eyes as big as dustbin lids, large shiny yellow eyes. Its huge head was full of foul teeth, and it had a long spiny tail like a whiplash."

"Tell me," said Mr Bikie, "when we first saw the submarine coming up from under the water in the cave, and you said 'it's him'. Did you mean the Loch Ness Monster?"

McTavish looked at him dismissively.

"You think I'm crazy, don't you laddie? When I said 'it's him' I meant Von Heinrich. I've been diving all my life laddie. Do you not think I know the difference between a submarine and the Loch Ness Monster? Besides, Nessie in Gaelic means 'Female of the Ness'. She is a she."

"My apologies," said Mr Bikie, realising that McTavish was getting agitated, "please continue."

"Well," said McTavish, "the creature got hold of me with its slimy tail, crushing me until I thought my eyes were going to pop out my head. Its terrible eyes stared down at me as it drew me towards its huge mouth. I thought it was going to bite me in half there and then but it hadn't finished with me just yet. It dived down to the bed of the lake and dashed me against the bedrock. That's when my leg was shattered. Then it dragged me out of the cave and into the loch. It was going to devour me. I'm sure of that. But fortunately for me a boat was passing overhead. The creature discarded me like a rag doll and then dived out of sight into the depths at great speed. Barely alive, I managed to swim to the shore. I haven't dived again from that day to this."

Mr Bikie took a sip of his beer. If what McTavish had told him were true, who could blame him for not wanting to dive again?

"Tell me," said Mr Bikie, "did your great-grandfather leave you any kind of clue as to where in the cave the treasure might be hidden?"

McTavish took an old leather wallet from his pocket and produced a small piece of paper that had yellowed with age. He slipped the paper across the table to Mr Bikie, who unfolded it carefully. A map perhaps he thought, but he was wrong.

Scrawled in black ink was a short riddle, handwritten in German.

> Unter der Burg
> Wo der Monster lauert
> Folge dem Wasser
> Eins. Zwei. <u>Drie</u>.

Mr Bikie translated it out loud. "Under the castle. Where the monster lurks. Follow the water. One two <u>three</u>."

Mr Bikie looked disappointed. "Is that it?" he said. "Is this all you have?"

"That's it," confirmed McTavish. "Four short lines and I've spent a lifetime trying to decipher exactly what they mean."

"But you must have some idea?" queried Mr Bikie. "I mean this bit about the castle where the monster lurks. That can only mean Urquhart Castle. But what about following the water? And why is only the number three underlined?"

"I have a theory about that," said McTavish, producing another piece of paper. He unfolded it and spread it out across the table. This time it was a map. "After a few years of searching in vain, I decided to use proper surveying techniques. I made this map, and then superimposed a grid reference. That way I could search each section thoroughly one at a time. It was then that I noticed a pattern."

"Yes?" said Mr Bikie, leaning forward to examine the map.

"You see," pointed out McTavish, "this is the first cave - the one with the pictographs in it. Then there's Nessie's Cave - the one with the waterfall. And finally, there's the one that leads up to the castle dungeons. You see - One Two Three. The three caves. The only question is which one of these caves is the underlined number three? Which one in the verse contains the treasure?"

Mr Bikie thought back to the drawings depicted on the cave wall. Something had been bothering him. There was no altar in Nessie's Cave. The stone altar depicted in the ancient drawings was missing.

"Look," said Mr Bikie, pointing to the map. "The cave that leads to the castle is no more than a wide tunnel." He paused for thought. "Supposing there's another cave? One you haven't discovered yet?"

"That's impossible," asserted McTavish. "I told you, I have surveyed every inch of those caverns. There's no other cave down there, you can be sure of that."

Mr Bikie thought back to the metal ring that had been placed in such a curious position on the side of the bridge.

"You said that Von Heinrich was a mountaineer," said Mr Bikie. "Have you checked around the walls in Nessie's Cave, above the lake, rather than under it?"

McTavish looked irritated and took a deep mouthful of his beer. He banged the glass down on the table. "I'm a diver, not a flipping mountaineer!" he said angrily, "No correction, I'm not even a diver anymore!" He struck on his crippled leg with his clenched fist for a second time.

Mr Bikie could feel the sudden change of mood. It made him wonder what tensions had existed between McTavish's great-grandfather and Baron Von Heinrich all those years ago. But McTavish apologised.

"I'm sorry," he said pulling himself together. "It's been a bit difficult for me since my accident." He paused for a moment. "I've never divulged anything about this to anyone before but... but I trust you MJ. I know you will help me."

He looked earnestly into Mr Bikie's eyes. "You will help me won't you laddie? Now that you know the whole story, you'll still help me won't you?"

Mr Bikie looked at him squarely, not knowing how he would reply. But once again the words tumbled from his mouth before his brain had time to properly engage. "Of course I'll help you McTavish. Of course I will!"

McTavish stood up and thrust an open palm across the table towards Mr Bikie. "Partners," he said enthusiastically, a broad smile spreading across his face.

Mr Bikie regarded McTavish's outstretched hand. "You never let me finish. There are conditions."

McTavish slumped back down into his chair. "Conditions, what conditions?"

"That if we find the hidden treasure, we hand it over to the proper authorities," responded Mr Bikie.

McTavish regarded Mr Bikie with disbelief. "Hand it over!" he spluttered. "Hand it over! I've spent a lifetime looking for that treasure. My lifetime! I'm not going to hand it over. You must be crazy!"

"Those are my conditions. If we find the treasure, we hand it over to the authorities. Take it or leave it," said Mr Bikie resolutely.

McTavish squirmed in his seat. Mr Bikie could imagine what was going through his mind. Without his help, McTavish might never find the treasure. His lifetime's dream would never be realised. Like his father and grandfather before him, he would grow old and die without ever having set eyes on the treasure.

McTavish's head was bowed towards the table as he spoke, straining on every word. "Very well," he said slowly, "I agree to your conditions."

Mr Bikie offered him his hand across the table. "Let's shake on it then partner," he said.

McTavish stood up with the manner of a man who had finally being freed from some invisible chains. The broad smile crept back across his face and his eyes took on new hope. He took Mr Bikie's outstretched hand and shook it enthusiastically.

"Partners laddie," he said happily, "partners. So when do we get started?"

"I'll meet you at the cave entrance tomorrow morning at eight o'clock," said Mr Bikie. "We'll see what we can do about finding your treasure then shall we?"

"Eight o'clock it is then laddie."

McTavish looked delighted.

CHAPTER 14

IN SEARCH OF TREASURE

It was another fabulous summer's morning with uninterrupted blue skies stretching from horizon to horizon. Mr Bikie had just returned from one of his many trips to his secret warehouse. He loaded the last of his equipment aboard his newly acquired rubber dinghy then eased the craft past the *Highland Princess* and out into the loch.

As he reached deeper water, he opened up the throttle and roared across the loch towards the castle. He sighted a good landing spot just south of the castle and landed his craft against the rocky shoreline. Half an hour later, he had all his equipment stacked up neatly outside the entrance to McTavish's cave.

He settled down on the granite rock above the entrance and waited for McTavish to arrive. As he leaned back he could see his hang glider, still stranded in the tree, flapping around gently in the breeze. He would have to retrieve it at some point in the future.

McTavish arrived at ten to eight and the two men then set about carrying the equipment down the tunnel to McTavish's Cave. An hour later they had completed their task and Mr Bikie decided to take a second look at the pictographs adorning the cave walls. Meanwhile, McTavish took a seat at the table and produced a battered old aluminium thermos flask from his knapsack.

"Coffee?" he called over to Mr Bikie. "Or I have something

stronger if you prefer?"

"Coffee will be fine," called back Mr Bikie, as he walked around the cave, re-examining the pictographs.

Since his previous visit, he had given the drawings a lot of thought. This time he studied them in greater detail. He reached the pit at the far end of the cave and shone his torch down into the darkness. Then he focused on the roof above the pit. A large iron ring, similar to the one he had seen on the side of the bridge was driven into the ceiling. On this, he guessed, had once hung a block and tackle with which McTavish's great-grandfather and Baron Von Heinrich had lowered down their heavy old fashioned equipment. He walked back to the table and pulled up a chair, accepting the large mug of coffee that McTavish had poured him. He sipped the treacly black liquid politely.

"We'd better get going," he said, laying his mug back down on the table.

"Ready when you are laddie," replied McTavish, draining his own mug before pushing himself to his feet.

McTavish went down the pit first and after lowering down their equipment Mr Bikie joined him at the bottom of the shaft. They loaded up with as much as they could carry and started off down the tunnel. McTavish reached the bridge first and looked across its treacherous slimy span.

"It's going to be a devil of a job getting this lot over to the other side laddie."

Mr Bikie pointed down to the metal ring he had noticed earlier, hammered into the stone floor beside the bridge.

"We could use that," he said. "What if we rig up a rope slide and run our packs straight down into the cave onto the beach? That would save us a lot of time and hassle."

"Aye that's a great idea laddie," said McTavish. "I wasn't looking forward to crawling over that bridge with all this stuff!"

Mr Bikie rummaged around in one of the backpacks and took out a reel of rope. He threaded the end through the ring and tied it off securely. Then he threw the coiled rope over the side of the bridge. It disappeared silently into the abyss below.

"We'd better get what's left of the gear from the bottom of the shaft first," said McTavish, turning to make his way back up the tunnel.

"No," said Mr Bikie. "I'll go back and get the last of the stuff. You carry on down to the beach and retrieve the other end of that rope. Secure it to something and pull it tight. I'll give you a shout when the first load is ready to come down. I'll send you down some floodlights in the first batch. I want you to set them up and shine them onto the walls around the cavern. Once we've got all the gear down here, I'm going to abseil down the rope myself. I want to see if I can see anything as I'm descending."

"Abseil," said McTavish, looking over the side of the bridge. "Rather you than me laddie!"

"All part of the service!" smiled Mr Bikie cheerfully.

Mr Bikie headed back up the tunnel and McTavish crouched down on all fours, ready to make his perilous crossing of the bridge. Once safely over to the other side, he followed the tunnel down to the beach and lit some old paraffin lamps which he hung on hooks around the walls. He retrieved the end of the rope from the edge of the lake and secured it to a large rock. Then he sat down on the rock and waited for Mr Bikie's return.

Reaching into his coat pocket he produced his tin of rolling tobacco and started to slowly and methodically roll himself a cigarette. All the time he kept a wary eye on the surface of the lake and his mind wandered back to the time he had been attacked by the monster in this very place. Finally he heard a shout from above and struggled to his feet.

"I'm ready when you are laddie," he shouted back, peering up into the dimly lit bell-shaped cavern. He grabbed hold of the rope and pulled it tight, waiting for the first load to be delivered. Up above Mr Bikie clipped on one of the bundles and pushed it over the side. It whirred down the rope gathering speed as it went. McTavish caught it and unclipped it at the other end.

Once all the bundles had been dispatched, Mr Bikie put on his climbing harness and clipped himself onto the rope. Down below McTavish was busy setting up the floodlights.

Mr Bikie eased over the edge and lowered himself down into the cavern – uncertain as to what he was looking for. He reached a point level with the top of the waterfall and paused to marvel at the torrent of water as it gushed out of the rock face. It cascaded down into the black waters below before forming a beautiful rainbow mist that bathed in the glare of the floodlights that McTavish had set up. He was about to move on when something caught his eye. There was something flapping around in the water at the top of the waterfall. Mr Bikie called over to McTavish, asking him to give him some slack on the rope.

McTavish watched as Mr Bikie started to swing back and forth across the lake, building up momentum, taking larger swings each time. McTavish realising what Mr Bikie was trying to do grabbed the end of the rope and pulled it back and forth in the manner of a bell ringer. Like a giant pendulum, suspended inside the casing of an oversized grandfather clock, Mr Bikie swung back and forth across the underground lake. With each successive swing, he moved closer to the top of the cascading waterfall.

He could see it now; it was a rope, a frayed old rope, dangling down from the roof of the river tunnel. He signalled for McTavish to take up the slack again and then abseiled down to meet him.

"Find anything laddie?" asked McTavish, eagerly.

"I think so," said Mr Bikie excitedly. "There's an old climbing rope flapping around in the water up there. It looks as though at some time in the past someone has followed that waterfall into the rock face."

McTavish clasped his hands together in delight. "Follow the water," he said, "just like the verse told us to."

Mr Bikie pointed across to a spot by the side of the waterfall.

"I'm going to swing over and try to land on that flat ledge over there. I'll make my way up to the mouth of the waterfall and explore the river course behind it. Let's see where it leads to shall we? You wait here for me and I'll be back as soon as I can!"

"Is there anything I can do to help you laddie?" asked McTavish.

"You can help to swing me across," replied Mr Bikie, not wanting McTavish to feel left out.

"Watch out for yourself over there laddie," said McTavish. "If you get into any trouble over there, I won't be able to follow you! Not up that rock face I won't."

"Don't you worry about me," said Mr Bikie. "I'll be okay!"

Mr Bikie reached into one of the backpacks and lifted out a climbing rope which he threw over his shoulder. Then he reached in again and produced a number of climbing pitons which he clipped on to his belt. He took hold of the rope and tied a piece of string around it; the other end of the string he tied to his belt.

McTavish started to swing him back and forth across the lake, and with expert timing, Mr Bikie let go of the rope and landed nimbly on the narrow ledge. He took a piton from his belt and hammered it into the rock face; then using the string he had attached earlier he pulled in the dangling rope and secured it to the piton. The rope would be there, ready and waiting for him on his return.

CHAPTER 15

FOLLOW THE WATER

Climbing up the rock face beside the waterfall was fairly straight forward. Crude footholds had been hacked into the rock and there were traces of rotting timber protruding out - all evidence of some ancient building activity.

Mr Bikie drew level with the waterfall and considered his next move. He climbed higher to a spot directly above the river tunnel and then lowered himself down to a point directly above the centre of the gushing water. He had clear sight of the river tunnel now.

On either side two narrow ledges had been cut into the sidewalls just above the water line. He tried to imagine why this had been done, and what had been here when the ancients had used these caves. He followed the line of sight from the right-hand side of the waterfall along the cavern wall and could just make out the almost invisible remnants of a wooden buttresses that had long ago rotted into the walls. The buttresses would once have supported a gangway running round the cavern walls before dropping down onto the beach. The spot where he now hung would have once housed a platform and the ledges inside the tunnel would have carried a wooden pathway, granting the ancients easy access to whatever lay beyond up the river tunnel.

At head height, running along the right-hand ledge of the river tunnel, he could see the now familiar iron rings stretching back until they were lost from sight. This relatively modern addition had no doubt been put there by Baron Von Heinrich to form a rope rail. The rope now lay in tatters and would need to be replaced. He climbed back across the rock face and lowered himself down to a point adjacent to the tunnel opening.

From the other side of the lake, McTavish looked on anxiously as Mr Bikie slowly edged himself, spider-like, into the mouth of the river tunnel. He reached the ledge and started to thread his rope through the rings, renewing the rail as he went.

After a while, he paused and looked back in the direction he had just come from. The light of the cavern was no longer visible, and in this cold, dark, dank place he felt very much alone. Over the past few days, McTavish had proved to be a good companion and, had it been possible, he would have liked to have had him with him now.

The tunnel started to widen, and as it did so the river flow eased. He stepped into the water and battled on up the river by foot.

Up ahead the tunnel split into tributaries. Mr Bikie followed the rope rings and took the tributary to the left. The tunnel split again, but this time only one of the tunnels carried water. The other tunnel was bone dry and could be accessed by three tall steps that led out of the water.

Three steps leading to a third cavern, thought Mr Bikie to himself. His pace picked up now, and his sense of anticipation heightened with every step. The tunnel rose steadily at first but then started to drop again, becoming wider and more rectangular as it did so. He took his last few paces out of the tunnel and entered a vast new cavern.

The underground cavern he now found himself in dwarfed anything he had previously seen. Half way along a magnificent glittering beach, against which lapped a massive lake, stood the large stone altar; the one he had seen depicted on the walls of McTavish's Cave. He had found the place of sacrifice. He had found the true home of the Loch Ness Monster!

There was something at the far end of the beach - something that looked out of place. His torch led him along the shoreline and as he passed the sacrificial altar he felt the evil embedded within the stone. As he closed in on the object at the end of the beach he realised what it was. It was a very rusty looking diving compressor with two air hoses leading out from it. The hoses trailed down to the water's edge before disappearing into the depths of the underground lake.

He had found McTavish's great-grandfather and Baron Von Heinrich. At the end of those lines, he had no doubt that he would also find McTavish's lost treasure.

Mr Bikie made his way back down the tunnel - he could hardly wait to tell McTavish of his discovery.

McTavish, who had been anxiously waiting his return, greeted him on the beach.

"Well laddie? Did you find anything?"

"Yes," said Mr Bikie triumphantly. "I've found it!"

"What? You mean the treasure?"

"Well yes and no," replied Mr Bikie. "Not the treasure exactly. Not yet anyway. But I have found another cavern and it's huge, absolutely vast. It makes this cavern look tiny in comparison. And what's more, it's got that sacrificial altar beside another vast underground lake. It's the cavern depicted on the walls of your cave McTavish. It's the true home of the Loch Ness Monster!"

McTavish's eyes widened with excitement.

"I'm afraid I also have some bad news though," added Mr Bikie.

"Bad news? What sort of bad news?"

"I'm sorry to tell you that I also found your great-grandfather and Baron Von Heinrich, or at least what is left of their equipment. Their air lines are trailing down into the water. I think they were probably involved in some sort of diving accident."

McTavish staggered back a few paces and sat down heavily on a rock, and to Mr Bikie's astonishment he started to weep. He wept for his great-grandfather; he wept for his grandfather, his father, and for himself.

"All those years," he cried. "All those wasted years. Looking - searching in the wrong place. What price have my family had to pay for this treasure, what price?"

Mr Bikie was taken aback. He had expected McTavish to be jubilant that he had found the treasure. But then he reflected on McTavish's words and realised that the search for the treasure had brought him and his family nothing but shattered dreams, untold troubles, injury and even death. It had been nothing but a curse on three generations of his kinfolk.

"I have to see this place!" cried McTavish standing up. "I have to see the place I have searched for all my life!"

Mr Bikie looked over to the waterfall. "I'm sorry McTavish, but you won't be able to make it up that rock face - you said so yourself."

"Damn blast this leg of mine," cursed McTavish. "I must see it I tell you. I have to see it!"

Mr Bikie looked back across to the waterfall. He could only imagine how important this must be for McTavish.

"Well," said Mr Bikie slowly, "I suppose I could rig up some sort of a pulley system. Maybe a rope chair or something like that. That might work."

"Now you're talking laddie, I know you can do it! I saw you climbing over there earlier. If anyone can get me up that waterfall, it's you laddie!"

"Very well," said Mr Bikie, "let's give it a try. I'll take the rest of the gear up the river tunnel first, and then we'll see what we can do about getting you over there. What time is it now anyway?"

McTavish examined his watch. "Just after twelve," he replied.

"Good," said Mr Bikie. "It's early yet. We'll have your treasure by this afternoon McTavish. You mark my words. We'll have your treasure this very afternoon!"

McTavish could hardly contain himself.

"At last!" he exclaimed. "The treasure!"

CHAPTER 16

LURKING IN THE DEEP

Using the rope chair Mr Bikie had rigged up, McTavish hauled himself up to the mouth of the tunnel. As he drew level with the waterfall Mr Bikie pulled him in and he was able to grab hold of the rope rail before planting his feet firmly on the ledge. Mr Bikie tied off the pulley ready for their return.

They travelled along the narrow ledge until it came to an end, then dropped down into the fast flowing water. Mr Bikie could only admire McTavish's grit and determination as the old man grappled his way up the river bed.

As before, Mr Bikie took the left-hand fork at the river split, and they battled on together until they reached the place where the three steps led out of the water.

"Three steps!" said McTavish.

"Yes," replied Mr Bikie, "three steps and three caverns! I think that's why the number three was underlined in that verse you showed me. It had more than one meaning!"

McTavish nodded in agreement and as he did so Mr Bikie noticed that the elder man was starting to look tired.

"We'll take a short break here shall we," he said sitting down on the top step. McTavish sat down beside him.

"I'm not as fit as I used to be laddie," said McTavish, producing a tin of rolling tobacco from his coat pocket.

"That's the worst of it over," said Mr Bikie reassuringly.

"You know it's funny," said McTavish, as he produced his old fashioned paraffin cigarette lighter and torched the end of his roll-up. "We're so close to finding the treasure, and yet somehow I don't want to get there. Funny, isn't it? Maybe I've spent a lifetime searching for something that was all along just a dream. Who was it that said: 'It is better to travel than to arrive'?"

"Robert Louis Stevenson," replied Mr Bikie. "And what he actually said was 'It is better to travel hopefully than to arrive'. But you won't be disappointed McTavish. Robert Louis Stevenson has got it wrong this time. Wait until you see the real *Nessie's Cave*. It is an unbelievable sight. I've set up some lighting down there for you so that you can see it in all its glory. The treasure is down there all right. It can't be anywhere else."

"What about the monster!" said McTavish. "What happens if that creature comes back whilst you're down there?"

"I've thought about that," said Mr Bikie. "You were attacked in the other cave weren't you - the 'other Nessie's Cave' so to speak. So I think that there are many of these underwater caves dotted around the shoreline that open up into the loch. That's why all those scientists and Loch Ness Monster hunters can never find her. She's clever enough to hide in the caves when they're out there looking for her. I would have to be very unlucky if the creature were to come back to that particular cave when I'm down there. I think I'll be okay!"

"But it could come back!" said McTavish. "It could! After all, you said that you thought that this was its main residence. The place depicted on the stone walls in my cave."

"Well, we'll see," said Mr Bikie. "Monster or no monster, we had better get going."

McTavish struggled to his feet. "Let's get going then laddie! It's time for me to realise my dreams."

They struck out with McTavish leading the way.

McTavish's pace slowed when he saw a finger of light reaching out for him from the tunnel ahead. It was the glow from the lights that Mr Bikie had left behind in the cave. McTavish stepped out of the tunnel and stood there for a moment in a trance-like state.

"Well," said Mr Bikie, coming up beside him, "what do you think?"

"It's magnificent," declared McTavish. "I can't believe it... It's just so beautiful!"

"Come on," said Mr Bikie, "and I'll show you the air compressor. The rest of my gear is already down there at the shore."

The two men followed the shoreline along the beach, spellbound by the magnificence of their surroundings. They reached the air compressor and McTavish examined it in great detail.

"Well," asked Mr Bikie, "what do you think?"

"Type seven," said McTavish, as he unscrewed the fuel cap. "I've seen one or two of these in my time. They were still used in my younger days. Even then they were considered to be antiques. But they kept them in service because they were regarded as being so reliable."

He peered into the fuel tank. "Empty!" he declared. "Perhaps the poor beggars ran out of air when they were still down under. Funny that though!" remarked McTavish.

"Funny?" enquired Mr Bikie.

"Yes, odd."

"Why?"

"Two reasons really," explained McTavish. "Firstly this unit is designed to work on a single tank of fuel for six hours or more.

That's a long time to be under the water. Secondly - why two lines into the water? One of them should have been up here topside with the safety line, and to make sure that there were no problems with the compressor. I suppose..." continued McTavish, trying to answer his own question, "that the treasure was so heavy and bulky that it would take two of them to bring it to the surface?"

"There could be another explanation," said Mr Bikie.

"What's that?" asked McTavish.

"It could be that neither man trusted the other enough to leave one of them up here in charge of the air supply. The treasure could easily have been brought up in small batches."

"Poor blighters," said McTavish. "You mean that them not trusting each other might have been their undoing?"

"Could be," said Mr Bikie, reaching into his rucksack and unpacking his wet suit. "I'll get down there and take a look shall I? See what really happened."

"Here, let me help," said McTavish.

With McTavish's help, Mr Bikie was soon fitted out in his diving suit and McTavish strapped on his air tanks.

"I'll attach this safety line to you laddie," said McTavish. "You know standard line code do you?"

"Yes, I think so," replied Mr Bikie.

"We'd better run through it all the same," said McTavish.

"OK," said Mr Bikie, "It's one pull for stop isn't it?"

"That's right laddie. And two pulls for more line. Three pulls to take up the slack".

"And four or more to haul me up," finished Mr Bikie.

"That's right laddie."

"You know something," said McTavish. "I haven't had this much fun in years. I actually quite envy you going down there."

"Overcome your fear of diving then have you?" smiled Mr Bikie.

"I believe I might have done just that," replied McTavish. "It's been over six years now since I had my accident and time, as they say, is a great healer. Seeing you geared up like this, ready to dive, reminds me of all the happy times I've had in the past down there under the water. When this is all over laddie, I'd be privileged if you would accompany me on my first dive. I want to get out there and start diving again!"

"I'd be delighted to accompany you," said Mr Bikie, "and you'll be able to buy yourself some brand new diving equipment with all that money the treasure brings in."

"Money?" said McTavish. "I thought you said we were going to hand the treasure over to the authorities."

"And so we shall," said Mr Bikie. "But there's usually a finder's fee isn't there - ten percent I think is standard. Whatever it is, it will turn out to be a tidy sum!"

"Why you young rascal," said McTavish. "You mean that you knew that all along and you didn't tell me?"

"Well I didn't want to get your hopes up," replied Mr Bikie. "But now we're so close to getting the treasure, I thought it was only fair to let you know."

McTavish accompanied Mr Bikie down to the water's edge.

"Go on laddie," said McTavish, handing him his face mask, "go on down there and get us our treasure."

Mr Bikie pulled the mask down over his face and adjusted his head torch. McTavish made some final checks to his air supply and then Mr Bikie slid effortlessly into the black waters of the lake; he disappeared beneath the surface.

He followed the old air lines into the murky depths and soon his depth gauge read one hundred feet. Still, the old air lines trailed on down. At one hundred and fifty feet he reached the bed of the lake. The air hoses trailed off along the bedrock and he followed them, guessing that they were heading out towards the loch. After a short distance, the lines turned sharply to the right and then disappeared into what appeared to be a natural alcove. Mr Bikie followed. The alcove turned out to be occupied!

At the end of one of the lines, sprawled out across the silt covered floor, lay a body in an old fashioned diving suit. He swam over. The diver's air hose had been severed - cut cleanly through close to the point where it entered the suit. The other line ran to a second diver who was propped up against the alcove wall. A timeworn wooden chest lay in the middle of the alcove between them. Mr Bikie swam over to the diver propped up against the wall and peered in through the glass visor. The face of a white boned skeleton stared back at him.

Judging by the size and length of the suit, Mr Bikie guessed that this was the remains of Barron Von Heinrich. But there was something very disturbing about the skeleton filled suit. It had a knife protruding from its chest, and another knife clutched in its bony hand. Barron Von Heinrich's death had been anything but accidental!

No one would ever know which one of these two men had initiated their fatal exchange. But over a hundred years ago in this alcove, a deadly fight had taken place. A fight driven by greed! Greed had taken control of them, and greed had reaped its morbid reward!

Mr Bikie turned his attention to the wooden chest. He unclipped the metal clasps around the sides and slowly lifted the heavy lid. He was not prepared for what he saw inside the chest. He gasped as the lid fell fully open - it was empty - there was nothing there. Nothing at all!

Mr Bikie closed the lid - his sense of disappointment palpable. What was he going to tell McTavish? He had so foolishly raised his hopes, and now, instead of bringing him back treasure, he had to tell him that there was none!

He was about to leave the alcove when he spotted a shiny object lodged in the soft silty sand beside the chest. He leaned forward and picked it up. It was a diver's watch, not an old fashioned diving watch, but a brand new one. The strap was broken but it was still ticking away happily. Mr Bikie shone his torch around the chest. There were footprints in the sand, not his footprints, but definitely recent, very recent indeed. It looked as though Von Heinrich had beaten him to the treasure. Perhaps only by a matter of minutes, but the prize had fallen to him.

With a heavy heart he made his way out of the alcove. He pulled the rope three times to signal for McTavish to take up the slack and followed the old air lines back in the direction he had come. He was deep in thought. So deep in fact that he failed to notice something looming up behind him.

Too late he felt its presence. He turned and his eyes widened with fear as he let out an involuntary scream of terror. Two giant yellow eyes stared down at him. He kicked out with his flippers in an attempt to make a dash for the surface, but the creature's tail whipped round and encircled him. He gave out a cry of pain as the creature's spiny flesh bit into his own; its crushing grip on his rib cage was unbearable. The creature swung him round to examine its prey. In a last desperate attempt to break free he drew out his diving knife and plunged it repeatedly into the monster's spiny tail. But the blade had little or no effect on such an enormous creature.

Up above on the beach, McTavish watched in horror as bubbles of escaping air rose to the surface from far below. He started to frantically pull in the lifeline, but he knew by the weight of the rope that the other end was no longer attached. He cried out in dismay as the severed end of Mr Bikie's lifeline surfaced.

"The monster!" he cried. "The monster has got him!"

He knew what would happen next. He had already lived through it himself. The monster would drag Mr Bikie out to the loch, just as it had done to him. He hurried along the beach and out of the cavern. He had to get up to the shoreline. It was his only hope. But in his heart, he knew that Mr Bikie would surely perish.

Down below the monster tightened its deadly grip. Mr Bikie's face mask imploded - water taking the place of oxygen. He continued to fruitlessly thrust his knife into the creature, but his lungs had now filled with water. A new calm came over him. The creature had won - the struggle was over! Slowly in the creature's deadly embrace they floated down to the bottom of the lake. He felt something pressing against his back and there was a flash of light as though his brain had exploded inside his head. Unconsciousness would soon take over. Then blackness fell upon him - blissful, comforting, blackness.

CHAPTER 17

THE CAPTURE OF MCTAVISH

"Come back here," shouted Wee Johnny's mother as he ran across the castle grounds.

"No Mummy, I have to help him. He's hurt."

Wee Johnny ran as fast as he could to where Mr Bikie lay on the grass; his bike lay beside him.

"Come back here," shouted his mother again giving chase – she was angry now.

Wee Johnny reached Mr Bikie and knelt down beside him. His mother, panting heavily, caught up and looked down at Mr Bikie in disgust.

"It's that crazy man again. He's got himself drunk and has fallen off his bike. And this time he's dressed himself up as a diver. Come away from him Johnny."

"No Mummy. You don't understand. He really is a diver and he's been drowned!"

"Drowned? What do you mean drowned? He can't be drowned; we're nowhere near the water. Now come away from him. I'll tell the man up at the ticket office and he'll come down here and sort him out. Now come away before I get really angry."

"No Mummy, I can't leave him. I can save him. I've read about it. I can save him. It's called Cardiopulmonary Resuscitation."

"Cardio... what?" asked his mother, "What do you mean you've read about it?"

But wee Johnny took no notice. He knew that time was of the essence. He carefully removed Mr Bikie's mask and turned his head to one side. Water started to drain from his mouth and nose. Then interlocking his hands he placed both of them on Mr Bikie's chest and started to administer chest compressions. Every so often he paused and blew twice into Mr Bikie's mouth.

"Come on MJ," he cried.

Wee Johnny's mother looked on in bewilderment and disbelief as Wee Johnny continued the chest compressions, talking to Mr Bikie all the time.

"Come on MJ," he cried, "we can do this! Come on MJ... Please MJ!"

On the third cycle of compressions Mr Bikie started to splutter. With all his might, Wee Johnny pushed him over onto his side and more water spewed out of the stricken Mr Bikie.

Wee Johnny lowered his head and whispered into his ear.

"You'll be all right now MJ. I'm sorry but I have to go. Your friend is down at the loch. I saw him with the monks."

Wee Johnny's mother had had enough. She grabbed Wee Johnny by the arm and dragged him away.

"I told you there was nothing wrong with him," she said. "He is just a disgusting drunkard."

As his mother dragged him away, Wee Johnny turned and gave a little wave. But Mr Bikie was in no fit state to respond. He felt sick, very sick. His body convulsed as streams of pain rippled through him. Everything appeared green to him. As his vision improved he focused on two tiny eyes staring up at him. The grasshopper eyed him curiously before continuing its journey across the lawn. He sat up and looked around confused. His bike lay beside him and he remembered the flash of light he had seen just before he had lost consciousness.

His mind was starting to clear. There was something someone had just said to him. It was ringing in his ears and he knew it was important. But what was it? He tried to repeat it to himself.

'Your friend is down at the loch. I saw him with the monks.'

Then everything came flooding back.

"McTavish!" he cried out loud. "The monks have captured McTavish!

He rose to his feet and sat astride his bike. With new found strength he peddled furiously across the castle grounds. As his bike reached the cover of trees there was a blinding flash and he was gone.

———

High up on the monastery's tower the warm wind breezed through his hair as he looked out over the loch. He propped his bike against the parapet wall and covered it with an old piece of discarded tarpaulin before crossing over to the heavy wooden door that exited the tower. The door creaked open to reveal a spiral staircase that led down into the main body of the monastery.

He closed the door behind him quietly, and proceeded with caution down the spiral staircase. He could hear voices now, growing louder with every step. Half way down the staircase a hallway broke off to the right. The voices were coming from a room at the far end of the corridor. The occupants sounded as though they were in high spirits, no doubt celebrating their recent success. There was the ting of a glass alerting everyone that a speech was about to follow. Mr Bikie edged his way along the hallway, closer to the half-open door. The occupants in the room fell silent as the booming voice of Von Heinrich filled the room.

"Well gentlemen, let's raise a glass to the success of our enterprise!"

"To success!" toasted the monks raising their glasses high and clinking them together.

Von Heinrich continued. "The treasure is ours and divers are completing their final task as I speak. Shortly we shall depart this fair land. You know the plan comrades. We meet in Denmark in 48 hours."

There was another toast and more merriment from the room. Mr Bikie retreated back down the hallway. There was not much time, they would be leaving shortly. He continued down the spiral staircase. Every so often a narrow window slit on the outer wall cast light into the stairwell. One of the narrow slits stood out from the others as it faced inwards towards the building. He paused to look through and was given an eagle's eye view of a large banqueting hall.

There were two chairs in the middle of the otherwise empty hall and on them sat two men bound from head to foot. He recognised McTavish immediately, but he couldn't quite see the face of the other man as his head was bowed towards the floor, but there was something familiar about him. And then he realised what it was. It was the same man that he had spotted on the hill above the *Highland Princess*; the man who was spying on him. It was PC Lockum the village policeman. The monks must have seen him, and mistakenly thought that he was spying on them.

He carried on down to ground level and reached the monastery's imposing entrance hall. A huge set of double doors to his right led into the banqueting hall. He gingerly pushed the wooden doors open and stepped through. Lockum's eyes narrowed towards him as he walked in.

"I wondered when you would turn up Bikie," he snarled. "I knew you were behind this all along!"

"Don't be silly man!" replied Mr Bikie pulling out his knife and moving towards them. "I'm here to help you!"

Lockum flinched at the sight of the knife, but Mr Bikie only wanted to cut his bindings free. He went behind McTavish first and released his hands before doing the same for Lockum. Then he moved round to the front and cut Lockum's legs free. As he knelt down to cut through McTavish's leg bindings he saw something in McTavish's eyes that alarmed him. But before McTavish could cry out in warning Lockum pounced; grabbing Mr Bikie round the neck and thrusting his arm up behind his back, forcing him to drop the knife to the floor.

"So you think you can fool me do you Bikie?"

As the two men wrestled with each other, McTavish shuffled his chair across the floor and reached down for the knife. He frantically started to cut through his own leg bindings.

There was a loud crash as the banqueting hall doors slammed open and Von Heinrich stormed into the hall with his men.

"Gentlemen, gentlemen, please, there is no need for violence."

At that moment McTavish managed to free himself from his bindings and he didn't hesitate; he made a mad dash towards one of the side doors that led out of the banqueting hall and into the kitchens.

"Get him!" snapped Von Heinrich.

Two of his men peeled off in pursuit. McTavish was no match for their speed and agility but he reached the door first. Slamming it shut behind him he turned the key in the lock.

Without further instruction, Von Heinrich's men ran back up the banqueting hall and through the double doors into the front hall. They were planning to cut him off in the grounds.

"Don't worry," said Von Heinrich smirking at Mr Bikie. "He won't get far! They'll get him!"

"Now enough of this convivial conversation," he said turning towards his men.

He pointed at Lockum. "That one," he said, "take him to the boat. He'll make a good hostage. We'll feed him to the fish later."

Two of Von Heinrich's men grabbed Lockum and started to frog march him out of the room. He struggled against his captors, shouting abuse at Mr Bikie as he was dragged off.

"You'll pay for this Bikie! You'll pay…!"

The shouting faded as he was marched down the main hall and out of the monastery. Von Heinrich turned his attention to Mr Bikie.

"Funny old world isn't it," he said. "You'd have thought he would have been grateful to you for trying to rescue him!"

"Now before you…" he paused looking for the right words, "…before you leave us there is something I want to ask you. Back there in the loch as my men were leaving with the treasure, they saw that creature swimming into the cave. Later, we found your friend on the shoreline looking for you. How did you manage to escape that monster?"

A shot rang out from outside.

"No matter, it's of no importance. That will be your friend," smiled Von Heinrich. "I told you he wouldn't get far." He turned to one of his men.

"Please be kind enough to show our guest upstairs Weasel."

"Upstairs?" queried Weasel.

"Yes," replied Von Heinrich, "to the tower! Our friend here might enjoy the little show I've arranged for him. It will be starting soon!"

"It will be a pleasure," sneered Weasel, his face twisting as he realised Von Heinrich's meaning.

"I'm going over in the sub," continued Von Heinrich. "The others are taking the boat. I'll send the boat back for you shortly." He turned to Mr Bikie.

"Well it's been a pleasure to have met you Mr Bikie. I'm sure my friend here will take good care of you!"

Von Heinrich turned and breezed out of the room with his men flanking him.

"Well it's just you and me now," smirked Weasel, bowing in a sarcastic manner and gesturing with his gun. "After you, please."

They walked through the main hall and started up the spiral staircase to the tower. Mr Bikie had one glimmer of hope; Weasel was leading him back to his bike. But what had Von Heinrich meant about a show starting soon? He decided to ask.

"Why are you taking me to the tower? What did Von Heinrich mean when he spoke of a show?"

"You'll find out soon enough," scoffed Weasel. "All you need to know for now is that when the show is over, so are you! So shut up and keep moving!"

They reached the door at the top of the spiral staircase.

"Open it," commanded Weasel, shoving the point of his gun into Mr Bikie's back.

Mr Bikie opened the door and they stepped out onto the tower.

"Over there," ordered Weasel, waving with his gun.

Mr Bikie walked over as directed, then turned and leant against the parapet wall. He could see his bike covered by the tarpaulin on the far wall. But Weasel was barring his way.

"It's time for us to part company I'm afraid," sniggered Weasel, raising his gun.

"Wait," said Mr Bikie, trying to buy time. "I thought Von Heinrich said there was going to be some sort of show?"

"I don't have time for Von Heinrich's little fantasy games," replied Weasel. "When that boat comes back, I'm going to be down there waiting for it, not standing around here waiting for some extravagant show!"

He raised his gun again, and this time his eyes were vacant. There was something empty and inhuman in that gaze. Mr Bikie braced himself for the impact of the bullet, when unexpectedly, Weasel lowered his gun again.

"No wait! I want to tell you first. It would give me great pleasure to let you know before you die. If you look up the Loch in that direction, there's soon going to be an explosion, a very big explosion. The divers have planted a limpet mine under the hull of your boat, and any moment now - boom! It's going to blow your boat and your family to kingdom come!"

He laughed hysterically like a crazed hyena.

"You're mad," said Mr Bikie.

"No, not mad," snarled Weasel, "just thorough. No witnesses you see!

You can thank Von Heinrich for this!"

He levelled his gun again.

"Goodbye Mr Bikie!"

CHAPTER 18

GOODBYE PRINCESS

McTavish locked the door behind him and hobbled down the corridor that led to the kitchens. He entered, seeking desperately for somewhere to hide. No, they would find him in here and he had no intention of being captured again. He charged through and burst out of the door at the far end of the kitchen only to find himself in a covered walkway. He was in the cloisters of the monastery.

Left or right? Either way could prove fatal. He chose to turn left and made his way down to the end of the arched terrace. Then he followed another terrace to the right. At the end of that terrace he was met by a wrought iron gate that led out into the gardens. It was bolted. In a panic he shook the gate vigorously before finding the latch bolt and sliding it open. He passed through quickly and headed for the final gate that would take him out of the monastery grounds and out on to open land. He hurried down the path towards it; he could smell freedom now.

But that was far from reality as he was running into a trap. As he burst through the gate and out onto the heathland he saw Von Heinrich's men closing in on either side of him.

Their prey in sight, Von Heinrich's men walked slowly towards each other, meeting in the middle as McTavish continued his futile attempt to escape.

"That's right old man," snarled one of them. "Run!"

They laughed as one of the men raised his gun and fired.

McTavish stumbled and crashed down into the heather as the bullet whizzed over his head.

"Did you get him?" asked one of the men.

"Of course I got him. I'm a crack shot aren't I?"

"Yes but we'd better just check to be sure. You might have just winged him."

McTavish lay very still, hardly daring to breathe. He could hear every word they were saying.

"You waste your time if you want to. I told you. I'm a crack shot. I got him right in the back of the head. You check if you want to. I'm getting out of here. The cops are going to be all over this place when that boat blows up!"

"I wouldn't worry about that," said the other man. "The cops will take ages to figure out what's been going on around here. By that time we'll be long gone. All we have to do now is drop the fuel off for the boys in Cove, and then we're on our way to Denmark."

"That can't be soon enough for me," said the other man, "now let's get out of here!"

McTavish breathed a sigh of relief as the two men turned and walked back towards the monastery. He had heard all he needed to. They were going to blow up the *Highland Princess* and with it Mr Bikie's family. He struggled to his feet and started to run across the heather towards the wood. Eventually, he came across the path that would lead him to the bay where the *Highland Princess* was anchored. He had no time to lose!

———

A game of Cluedo was in full swing on the *Highland Princess* and the radio was playing away happily in the background.

"It's your turn," said Sprocket.

Spindle looked towards the heavens for inspiration before she spoke. "I think it was Colonel Mustard, in the library, with the candlestick," she said.

"Nope," said Sprocket. "You lose!" he rolled the dice. "I think it was Miss Scarlet, in the kitchen, with the lead pipe."

"Wrong again," said Mrs Bikie, picking up the dice.

"Shh..," said Spindle, raising her finger to pursed lips. "Did you hear that?"

"What?" asked Sprocket.

Mrs Bikie stood up and turned off the radio. Scottie gave a long low growl.

"Quiet Scottie," said Spindle. They all fell silent.

"I can hear something," said Mrs Bikie. "It sounds like someone is shouting. Wait here and I'll go up on deck and take a look."

Dusk was starting to fall as she looked across the bay to the shore. A scruffy old man wearing a heavy trench coat was standing on the beach shouting and waving frantically in her direction. To her surprise, the old man took off his heavy coat and threw it to the ground before wading into the water. He kept shouting something all the time, but Mrs Bikie couldn't quite make it out. He seemed to be shouting something about a bomb. Yes, that was it; he was shouting that there was a bomb on board. She couldn't imagine how that was possible but she wasted no time and ran back down below to the galley.

"Get your coats children," she ordered. "Quickly, we have to get out of here and into the dinghy."

Sprocket and Spindle had no idea what was going on but they knew from their mother's tone that there was something seriously amiss. Spindle grabbed hold of Scottie and they all went up on deck before jumping into the small rubber dinghy.

The old man had started to swim towards them, and as they reached the halfway point he came up alongside and addressed Mrs Bikie.

"I'm a friend of MJs," he said, trying to catch his breath. "You've got to get out of here - a bomb has been placed under your boat. It's going to blow up at any moment!"

Mrs Bikie looked down at the scruffy half-drowned stranger. "Sprocket," she said, "help me get him out of the water."

With great difficulty, they managed to drag McTavish into the dinghy. McTavish took hold of one of the oars and with Mrs Bikie on the other they rowed frantically towards the shore. They all piled out of the dinghy as soon as it hit the beach.

"Run," shouted McTavish urgently. "Quickly run!"

It was the flash from the explosion that hit them first, the heat burning into their backs as they ran up the beach. Their ears popped painfully as the shock wave picked them up and threw them to the ground like rag dolls. Debris showered down on them from above and they all covered their heads with their arms as a means of protection.

An eerie silence followed. But as their ears readjusted they could hear the sound of crackling flames, and they looked up to see the *Highland Princess* burning in the bay.

"Everybody all right?" asked Mrs Bikie anxiously.

Wordlessly they nodded, transfixed by the sight of the *Highland Princess* enveloped in flames - they could feel the heat from the fire burning into their faces.

"Where's MJ?" asked Mrs Bikie turning to McTavish.

"I left him back at the monastery," replied McTavish. "It's all my fault!"

"What do you mean it's your fault? What has happened to MJ?"

"I should never have got him involved in all this. I'm afraid I have some terrible news for you."

"What news?" asked Mrs Bikie, fearing his answer.

"He was captured by the monks when he came to rescue me. I managed to escape, but on my way here I heard shots coming from the monastery. More than one shot... several. I think the monks... I think the monks have killed him!"

They all stared at McTavish in disbelief as they tried to take in what he had just said.

Sprocket spoke up.

"We saw a monk yesterday mum. He was on the cliff path at the end of the beach. He must have followed us here. I'm sorry mum I should have told you."

Mrs Bikie jumped to her feet.

"OK children. I want you to stay with Mr..." she looked down at McTavish.

My name is McTavish," he replied. "Hamish McTavish."

"With Mr McTavish," continued Mrs Bikie, "I'm going to find your father."

And with that she started running along the beach towards the path that led to the monastery.

CHAPTER 19

ESCAPE FROM THE TOWER

Weasel pulled the trigger but the weapon failed to discharge. He cursed loudly and expertly racked the slide ready to pull the trigger again. But it had given Mr Bikie the vital second he needed to make a dash for it. He plunged through the door at the top of the staircase and slammed it behind him. As he spiralled down the stairwell, shots rang out, ricocheting off the walls. The faster he spiralled down the dizzier he was becoming. Weasel lost his balance and tripped, crashing down the staircase, dropping his gun as he did so. He quickly retrieved it and resumed the chase.

Mr Bikie reached the main hall at the bottom of the staircase and staggered towards the exit. He plunged through the main door and darted across the grounds towards the heather. Weasel emerged from the monastery shooting wildly in his direction, but dusk was now well established and the bullets just whizzed past him harmlessly.

Weasel gave up the chase, more interested now in catching the boat Von Heinrich was sending back for him. He would tell Von Heinrich that he had killed Mr Bikie as instructed.

Mr Bikie joined the path and ran towards the bay where the *Highland Princess* was anchored. As he reached the highest point of the path he heard an explosion. A giant plume of smoke and fire lit up the evening sky. He paused, shocked with disbelief - then he ran even faster.

It was Mrs Bikie who saw him first, a familiar figure running down the path towards her.

"MJ!" she shouted, as she ran towards him.

As they met Mrs Bikie flung her arms around him and hung on tight.

"Where are the children?" asked Mr Bikie anxiously.

"They're safe," replied Mrs Bikie. "They're down on the beach with a man called McTavish. He says he knows you."

"McTavish!" exclaimed Mr Bikie. "McTavish is alive? I thought he was dead!"

"No," replied Mrs Bikie. "He swam out to our boat to warn us about the bomb. He saved us MJ. Without him we would have been killed. But he thinks you're dead MJ. He said he heard shots coming from the monastery and thought that the monks had killed you. What is this all about MJ? Why are those men trying to kill us?"

"It's a long story," replied Mr Bikie. He looked back up the path towards the monastery.

"We're safe now," he said. "I'll tell you all about it later."

Mrs Bikie noticed some blood running down the side of his face.

"You're hurt," she said, tracing the blood back to his ear.

Mr Bikie put his hand to the side of his head and felt the gooey soggy blood.

"One of the bullets must have nicked me," he said. "It's nothing, just a flesh wound."

When they reached the top of the path, high above the beach, they looked down on the *Highland Princess* burning in the bay.

"Such a wicked thing to do," said Mrs Bikie. "How could anyone do such a thing?"

Mr Bikie had no reply.

They reached the bottom of the path and walked along the

beach towards McTavish and the children. Scottie spotted them first and raced to greet them. The children jumped to their feet and chased after him, Scottie barking excitedly all the way.

"Daddy!" shouted Spindle, launching herself at him. "That man McTavish said you were dead!"

"He thought I was!" replied Mr Bikie.

They all walked along the beach to where McTavish was waiting for them.

"Thank you McTavish," said Mr Bikie. "Thank you for saving my family. I shall be eternally grateful."

McTavish's eyes twinkled in the light of the fire. "No problem laddie. I'm just delighted to see that you're still alive. I thought that you were a goner!"

"Likewise," replied Mr Bikie. "I thought the monks had killed you."

They all sat down on the beach and watched the *Highland Princess* as she burned in the bay. Finally, her bow lifted out of the water and she started to sink stern first. The water in the bay sizzled as she went down. In her final death throws she hissed loudly before disappearing under the water forever.

"Goodbye Princess," said Spindle sadly.

Scottie went over and tried to comfort her, resting his head on her lap. Spindle stroked his head gently.

"I don't think that man at the boatyard is going to be very pleased with us," she said to Scottie. "Not when he finds out what we've done with his boat!"

Mrs Bikie laughed first and the rest could not help but join in. Not just at Spindle's understated remark, but more so because they were alive - together and still alive!

CHAPTER 20

MCTAVISH'S CROFT

"Well, what now?" asked Mrs Bikie.

"You'll be my guests," said McTavish unexpectedly. He struggled to his feet and produced a small torch from his coat pocket. "I have a croft not far from here. Follow me."

They stood up and brushed the sand off their clothes before following McTavish along the beach - this time in the opposite direction to the monastery. At the far end of the beach, they joined a stony path that sloped up away from the loch. A full moon broke out of cloudless skies to help them find their way. After half a mile of steady ascent, the path levelled out and they entered a valley. In the distance through the twilight of the moon, they could see the outline of a small croft surrounded by a number of neglected old outbuildings.

"My croft," indicated McTavish.

They reached the front door of McTavish's croft and he bade them wait outside for a moment while he lit a lantern.

"No electricity in these parts," he explained.

Inside the croft, the main living area looked very austere and sparsely furnished. There was a couch against one wall and a large table in the centre, surrounded by a number of heavy wooden chairs. A wide chimney breast took up most of the far wall, under which stood an old fashioned cooking range. McTavish had dedicated another of the walls to framed photographs of various sea-going vessels that he had worked on over the years.

McTavish walked over to the cupboard next to the cooker range and opened it.

"I'm afraid I don't have much to eat," he said, looking at a single tin of broad beans and half a box of teabags. "No wait," he said reaching into the cupboard under the sink. "I have a few potatoes. I'll make you some potato and bean soup. My speciality!" he added light-heartedly.

Mrs Bikie turned her attention to the bullet wound that Mr Bikie had suffered.

"Do you have a medical kit by any chance McTavish?"

"That's something I do have," said McTavish, reaching into one of the cupboards. "Here we go." He handed Mrs Bikie a small white plastic box with a red cross on it.

Mrs Bikie cleaned the wound and half an hour later they were all gathered around the table tucking into some, surprisingly good, wholesome soup. McTavish had managed to find some stale old bread, which he had toasted on the griddle to make palatable.

"So how do you manage to get to work from here?" asked Mr Bikie, tipping up his bowl and spooning out the very last drop of soup.

"I don't," replied McTavish. "I only stay here on the occasional weekend nowadays. Most of the time I live in the staff block at the back of the hotel. Beth, one of the waitresses at the hotel, gives me a lift over here in her boat sometimes."

"Is that your sweetheart then?" asked Spindle cheekily.

"Spindle," said her mother sternly, "that's none of your business!"

McTavish, who had started collecting the plates from the table, chose to reply.

"Aye it's true she's caught my eye, right enough, but she would never fall for an old cripple like me." His eyes glazed over.

"Now that's quite enough children," said Mrs Bikie, "it's time that you two were off to bed. We have to be up early tomorrow morning and start our journey back home."

"Home!" protested Sprocket. "But we're supposed to be on holiday."

"I'm sorry children but the holidays are over. We have to go home, and that's all there is to it."

"Oh pants," said Spindle, crossing her arms petulantly.

Mrs Bikie was about to tell her off, but on this occasion she let it go. She knew how disappointed the children must be feeling.

"You're both sleeping in the spare room tonight," said Mrs Bikie. "Now do as you're told and go to bed. We'll be heading home at dawn. If you need us for anything, your father and I will be sleeping in here on the couch. We'll be quite comfortable in here."

She looked over at the couch, doubting her own words, before ushering Sprocket and Spindle out of the room. She returned shortly and resumed her seat at the table. Mr Bikie looked over to her.

"I'm just going to pop out for a breath of fresh air," he said. "I may be some time."

Mrs Bikie nodded to him knowingly as he stood up to leave.

"May I have a loan of your torch please McTavish?" asked Mr Bikie.

"Of course you can laddie," said McTavish, rummaging around in his coat pocket. "Here we go laddie."

Once outside Mr Bikie wasted no time and broke into a steady jog. The full moon lit his way and he soon reached the edge of the wood above the monastery. He paused momentarily to study the building before crossing the heather and joining the path to the main door. He slipped through and stood motionless in the dark, listening for anything that might indicate that the building was still occupied. Satisfied that he was alone, he flicked on his torch and set off up the spiral staircase to the tower. His bike was where he had left it leaning against the parapet. He removed the tarpaulin, sat astride his bike and was gone.

Mrs Bikie looked up with relief as he entered the croft, glad to see him return safely.

"McTavish has told me everything," she said from her seat at the table. "It sounds like you've had quite a day of it!"

"That's one way of putting it," said Mr Bikie, slumping down onto one of the chairs. "Any chance of a cup of tea please Marion?"

"Yes of course dear," replied Mrs Bikie. "I'll make us a fresh pot."

She crossed over to where the old fashioned copper kettle was simmering away happily on the hob. "I'm afraid there's no milk." It'll have to be black. Would you care for another cup of tea Mr McTavish?"

"Aye, that would be grand lassie," said McTavish, taking his tin of tobacco and placing it on the table in front of him. "But there's no need to be calling me mister. Everybody around here just knows me as McTavish."

"Okay, 'McTavish' it is then," she said, returning to the table with a couple of steaming hot mugs of tea.

McTavish finished rolling his cigarette and lit it with his flame thrower of a lighter. Mrs Bikie coughed and waved her hand around in the air, but McTavish didn't seem to notice.

"So where do you think Von Heinrich and his gang are now?" asked Mrs Bikie.

"I don't know," responded Mr Bikie, "but I overheard a conversation back in the monastery about them meeting up in Denmark in 48 hours time."

"I also heard something," said McTavish. "They said something about Cove. That they had to go there first."

"Cove?" said Mrs Bikie thoughtfully. "There must be hundreds of coves dotted around the coastline."

"No," said McTavish, "they specifically said 'Cove'. It must be an actual place name, not just any old cove."

"Do you have a map here by any chance?" asked Mr Bikie. "We could look it up in the index and see if it's listed."

"No, not in here," said McTavish, "but there'll be one outside in Bertha!"

"Bertha?" enquired Mrs Bikie.

"Yes Bertha," replied McTavish, "it's my old camper-van. I keep her in the barn. There should be a map in the glove compartment."

"You have a camper-van?" said Mr Bikie, sitting up with interest.

"Yes," replied McTavish, "but I haven't driven her for years. Not since my accident."

McTavish stubbed his cigarette out in the ashtray and stood up to leave.

"I'll get the map for you," he said.

"I'll come with you," said Mr Bikie reaching into his pocket for McTavish's torch.

The two men went outside and crossed the courtyard towards the barn. One of the barn doors was hanging half off its hinges.

"I'll have to fix this door some time," said McTavish, tugging away at it. Mr Bikie gave him a hand and they stepped inside.

In the middle of the barn stood a camper-van, covered in a large white linen sheet. McTavish brushed away the cobwebs and pulled back the linen cover to reveal Bertha.

"Do you think it still runs?" asked Mr Bikie, looking at her thoughtfully.

"Well she did when I laid her up," replied McTavish, "but that was years ago. You're welcome to try and start her if you wish. The keys are in the ignition."

Mr Bikie jumped into the driver's seat and turned the key. There were a couple of clicking sounds from under the bonnet but nothing else.

"It's dead!" declared Mr Bikie.

"The battery will be flat," said McTavish, riffling through the passenger glove compartment in search of the map. "Ah here it is!

They shrouded Bertha back under her linen cover before returning to the croft. Mrs Bikie was sitting at the kitchen table looking pensive. They joined her at the table and McTavish flicked through the pages of the map until he reached the index at the back. He squinted down at it.

"The writing is a wee bit small for me," he said as he rummaged in his coat for his reading glasses.

"Allow me!" said Mrs Bikie, reaching over and politely taking the map from McTavish.

"Cove... Cove... Cove...," she said, running her forefinger down the index. "Here we go, Cove. There are a few of them listed and there's one right here in the Highlands. Page forty-eight." She flicked back through the pages. "Ah here we are - it's over here on the West Coast."

"I don't think that'll be the one," said McTavish. "If they're heading for Denmark they're more likely to be heading for the East Coast."

Mrs Bikie turned back to the index.

"There's a 'Cove Bay' near Aberdeen. That's on the East Coast! And here's another one in the Scottish Borders."

"The Borders," said Mr Bikie.

"Yes, come to think of it I've heard of it before, I have an aunt who moved down there from Edinburgh years ago. I'd forgotten all about that. Aunty Agnes is her name. She wrote to me a few years back inviting me down there, but I've never really had the chance to take her up on her offer. She told me that in the olden days the place used to be infamous for smugglers and contraband, mostly coming in from the continent. I'll bet you that's the Cove they were talking about. That'll be where Von Heinrich and his gang have gone!"

"I think she's right," said McTavish. "It all makes sense. It would be one of the shortest crossings between Scotland and Denmark!"

"It's possible I suppose," said Mr Bikie. "But how would they get that sub of theirs all the way down there. They can't just sail her up through the Caledonian Canal in broad daylight can they?"

"Low loader," said McTavish. "That's the way we used to transport our diving subs around the place; by road. It can save you days, especially when you want to move a sub from one side of the country to another."

There was a lull in the conversation as they gave this due consideration.

"Let's go down there and see if we're right," said Mrs Bikie unexpectedly.

"Where, to Cove?" asked Mr Bikie, looking across the table at her.

"Yes, why not, we're still on holiday aren't we? Let's go there. Let's go to Cove!"

"We can't," said Mr Bikie, "it's too dangerous. Perhaps you've forgotten that those men tried to kill us! We can't put the children into harm's way like that, chasing around after a gang of thugs."

"Aunty Agnes will look after the children for us," reasoned Mrs Bikie. "They'll be safe with her. And the children will be thrilled to get the holiday we promised them!"

"I don't know," said Mr Bikie uncertainly.

But Mrs Bikie had already made up her mind, and she could see that Mr Bikie was weakening to the idea. He made one last attempt to fend her off.

"Anyway," he said, "we have no way of getting there!"

"We'll take Bertha," said Mrs Bikie.

"We can't," he replied, "the battery is as flat as a pancake."

"We'll push-start her then," declared Mrs Bikie. "Come on MJ. Let's go and find McTavish's treasure. You know that we can do it!"

Once again the words tumbled out of his mouth before his brain had had time to engage properly.

"Ok," he said, "let's do it. Let's go and find McTavish's treasure."

Mrs Bikie smiled broadly and raised her mug in the air. "Let's make a toast," she said. "Let's make a toast to the treasure!"

They all raised their mugs high in the air and clunked them together.

"To the treasure!" they cried.

CHAPTER 21

COVE

As dawn broke, Mrs Bikie drew open the children's curtains and the first rays of morning sunshine flooded the room.

"Wake up children. We're going on holiday!"

Sprocket sat up in bed, rubbing the tiredness from his eyes.

"I thought you said we were going home today mum?"

"I did, but there's been a change of plan. We're going to visit my Aunty Agnes in the Scottish Borders."

"Does that mean we're still on holiday?" asked Spindle sitting up excitedly.

"Yes it does," confirmed Mrs Bikie. "Aunty Agnes lives by the sea in a place called Cove. She's very nice. I used to stay with her in Edinburgh when I was a child. You'll like her."

Sprocket and Spindle wasted no time in getting dressed, and they were soon sitting at the breakfast table. McTavish had toasted the last of the stale bread and they nibbled away at it politely.

Mr Bikie had borrowed some old clothes from McTavish and the children laughed in glee when he appeared at the breakfast table wearing a dazzling multi-coloured Bermuda shirt and flared velvet trousers.

Once the laughter had subsided, Mrs Bikie told them about the camper-van and McTavish explained further.

"It's called Bertha," he said, setting aside his own inedible piece of toast. "She won't fire up at the moment, but we're going to try to push-start her."

"Push-start her?" questioned Spindle. "What does that mean?"

"It means you push her stupid," said Sprocket harshly. Spindle glared at him.

"We're hoping to push her to a point where the track drops down steeply," explained Mr Bikie. "McTavish and I will get her out of the barn first and we'll meet you outside when you're ready to go."

The two men crossed the yard and entered the barn. They pulled the linen cover off Bertha and Mr Bikie went round the back to push her. He pushed with all his might, but Bertha stayed glued to the spot.

"It's no use," he strained, "the brakes have seized!"

"Don't worry about that laddie," said McTavish. "I'll soon take care of that for you!"

With that, he walked over and took hold of a large sledge hammer that hung on the barn wall.

"Stand aside laddie," he said. "I'll soon have her freed up!"

McTavish went around each wheel in turn, striking his hammer squarely in the centre of each hub. Every time he did so, an audible click could be heard as the seized brakes sprung open. They both went round back and pushed. This time Bertha started to move and they kept pushing her until she was out of the barn and out into the courtyard.

Mr Bikie went back into the barn and re-emerged with his bike, which he had left there the night before. He started to strap it onto the tailgate of Bertha.

"Where did you get that from laddie?" asked McTavish looking puzzled.

"Found it when I was out for a walk last night," said Mr Bikie, in an attempt to explain its presence.

McTavish said no more, but Mr Bikie knew that he found this explanation suspicious.

The others emerged from the croft to join them.

"You jump in and steer McTavish," said Mr Bikie. "We'll do the pushing."

It was hard work pushing the heavy camper-van along the rough track, but eventually they reached the brow of a steep hill.

"Okay," called Mr Bikie to McTavish, "are you ready?"

"Ready when you are laddie," shouted back McTavish from the driver's seat.

They gave one last big push and Bertha set off bouncing down the rocky track, gathering speed as she went. McTavish put her into gear and slowly lifted his foot from the clutch. At first, Bertha coughed and spluttered, but then, as she neared the bottom of the hill, she burst into life and a huge cloud of white smoke belched out of her exhaust.

The Bikie family cheered enthusiastically and McTavish blew Bertha's horn triumphantly. They ran down the hill to join him.

"You drive laddie," said McTavish, stepping out of the driver's seat. Mr Bikie jumped in and took the wheel.

"All aboard," he shouted. And they all clambered on board excitedly.

Bertha set off down the stony track, rocking her occupants violently from side to side as she bounced along the rugged roadway. Mrs Bikie likened it to travelling inside a tumble drier. Eventually, they reached a minor tarmacked road.

"Which way now?" asked Mr Bikie.

"It's left here laddie," said McTavish from the back seats, "then first right. We join the main road just south of here."

Mr Bikie looked across to Mrs Bikie. "I hope your Aunty doesn't mind us dropping in unannounced like this?"

"She won't," replied Mrs Bikie. "We should get a mobile signal once we hit the main road. I'll give her a call and let her know we're on our way."

"How long will it take to get there?" asked Spindle.

"About five or six hours I expect," replied Mr Bikie.

"I'm hungry," complained Sprocket.

"I think we all are," said Mrs Bikie. "We'll stop at Pitlochry and get something to eat. How does that sound?"

There was universal approval at this idea.

When they reached Pitlochry, they all feasted on fish and chips. Spindle, having consumed a huge portion of fish, promptly fell fast asleep in the back.

"So," said Mr Bikie, "tell me about this aunty of yours? You've never mentioned her before."

"Oh, well, as I said, she used to live in Edinburgh where she had a huge house. We often visited her when I was a kid. She had some sort of big government job - in intelligence I think. We used to joke that she was some sort of spy. Who knows, maybe she was."

"She sounds fascinating," commented Mr Bikie.

The journey seemed to go on forever but finally they neared their destination. The camper-van veered hard left onto a minor country road, jolting Spindle from her sleep.

"Are we there yet?" she asked sleepily.

"We are," said Mrs Bikie. "You should see the village of Cove coming up any minute now."

Aunty Agnes lived at the far end of the village in a quaint old house perched high on the cliffs above the sea.

A warm-hearted, slightly plump woman met them at the door. She had a twinkle in her eye and as Mrs Bikie had expected, the children took an instant liking to her.

"Come away in dearies. Your rooms are ready for you. You'll find fresh towels on the beds and I've also looked out some fresh clothes for you. I'll look something out for your father as well," she said eyeing Mr Bikie's Bermuda shirt and flared velvet trousers. "Once you've had the chance to freshen up, I'll be in the kitchen waiting for you. I'm going to make you some homemade Scottish pancakes."

They came down in dribs and drabs, each taking their place at the kitchen table. Aunty Agnes served them hot pancakes straight from the griddle and they helped themselves to copious amounts of farmhouse butter and homemade jam.

"Can we go out and play now?" asked Sprocket, polishing off his third pancake.

"Yes, of course you can dearies," said Aunty Agnes. "There's a swing ball and a badminton set in the garden shed. It's open. Help yourself to anything you want out of there."

The children sprung to their feet and tumbled out of the kitchen door into the garden.

"Don't go anywhere near the cliffs!" called out Mrs Bikie after them in warning.

Aunty Agnes turned her attention to her guests.

"Well Marion, you said on the phone that you had been involved in some sort of trouble up there in Loch Ness? What terrible thing could have happened to make you cut your summer holidays short?"

Mrs Bikie told Aunty Agnes everything. McTavish even told her about the existence of Nessie's Cave and of the monster.

"I see," said Aunty Agnes, "so you think this Von Heinrich fellow and his gang are heading down here to Cove?"

"It's possible," said Mrs Bikie, "but we don't really know for sure."

Aunty Agnes looked across to Mr Bikie and McTavish.

"Why don't you boys go down to the local pub," she said looking up at the kitchen clock. "It will be opening shortly. You can find out most things that are happening in the village down there!"

McTavish looked over to Mr Bikie. "Sounds like a good idea to me laddie. I could murder a pint!"

"How far is it?" asked Mr Bikie.

"It's not far," replied Aunty Agnes, "you can't miss it really! It's called the *Smugglers Tavern*, and you'll find it close to the shoreline at the other end of the village."

"Okay," said Mr Bikie, looking at McTavish, "let's go shall we?"

"Remember and be back in time for your dinner!" shouted Mrs Bikie after them sternly. "Aunty Agnes is cooking us an extra special beef casserole."

"Don't worry," called back Mr Bikie, "we're only going to have a couple of pints!"

———

The salty sea air filled their nostrils as they took the winding cliff path towards the village. Strong winds had whipped the sea into a frenzy and they could hear the sound of waves crashing against the rocks far below. A storm was brewing up, and out to sea a rumble of thunder sent out its warning.

The *Smugglers Tavern* had just opened its doors and they were the first customers to arrive. They headed straight to the bar.

A heavily set bartender covered from head to foot in tattoos

130

stood behind the counter.

"What will it be gentlemen?" he asked in a pleasant manner.

"Two pints of your local ale please," said Mr Bikie, looking across to McTavish for confirmation. He nodded his approval.

"Two pints of 'Foul Fish Special' it is then sir!" said the barman pulling on one of the hand pumps.

They found a nice booth at the far end of the tavern and settled down to discuss the day's events.

The tavern was filling up fast now and after a couple more 'Foul Fish Specials', Mr Bikie and McTavish were starting to feel quite merry. Their conversation was interrupted by the sound of raised voices coming from the bar. Two fishermen were having an argument with the bartender.

"I told you boys the last time you were in here that there would be no more drink for you two until you've settled your bar bill. Now get out! You're welcome to come back when you've paid the money you owe me."

"We're good for it Patrick, you know we are," said one of the fishermen. "We're working on a big job just now and we'll be clearing all our debts soon."

"I've heard that all before," said the barman.

"Come on Patrick, just a couple of pints! Please..!"

The barman relented and reached under the counter for some glasses.

"Okay I'll do it this one last time. But don't bother coming back in here again unless you've got the money you owe me. Understand?"

The two fishermen took their drinks gratefully and made their way towards one of the booths next to were Mr Bikie and McTavish were sitting. McTavish had a feeling about them and laid his hand on

Mr Bikie's forearm. Mr Bikie understood and they fell silent. The two fishermen started to converse with each other.

"Well brother, we're in a fine state now aren't we? We don't even have enough money to buy a couple of pints!"

"We'll have plenty of money tomorrow once we've escorted that sub over the channel."

"I don't like it," said his brother. "We've done a few things in our time but nothing as dodgy as this!"

"Listen little brother! All we have to do is act as a tender to the sub until she's safely over to the other side. There's nothing dodgy or illegal about that, is there?"

"I guess not, but that was before they lumbered us with that bloke they brought with them! This is kidnapping you're getting us involved in. We could end up in jail for this."

"It's got nothing to do with us what happens to him. We simply have to deliver him to the rendezvous point. What they do with him after that is their business. Besides Von Heinrich has doubled the money we will receive."

"Double you say? That's a small fortune!"

"That's right little brother, a small fortune and it's all for us. It's about time we had a bit of luck around here."

"Do you still have him locked up in the *Herring House?*"

"No, I've moved him out of there into the *Cellars*. It's safer to keep him there, and still close enough to the *Creel Pot.*"

"What time do we leave?"

"We sail on the tide," replied his brother. "Von Heinrich and his men are using that ramp up in Dunbar to launch their sub. We have orders to rendezvous with Von Heinrich and Weasel two miles offshore."

"It's going to be a long night brother. We'd better get going."

The two fishermen drained the last of their pints and made their way out of the tavern.

"Did you hear that!" said McTavish. "They've got Lockum, right here in Cove!"

"I know," said Mr Bikie looking worried. "We've got to get him away from those two fishermen. After you escaped, back there in the monastery, Von Heinrich said that he was going to feed Lockum to the fish. I didn't realise he actually meant it!"

"Lockum deserves to be fed to the fish if you ask me!" said McTavish taking another slurp of his beer. "He almost got you killed back there in the monastery!"

"I know," said Mr Bikie, "but I think he's a bit confused at the moment. He doesn't know the difference between friend and foe."

Mr Bikie took a long drink of his beer. "I need to give this some thought," he said looking concerned.

McTavish looked over to the wall clock behind the bar. "We're late," he said urgently, "we'd better get back to the house for dinner, or we'll be the ones who are fed to the fish!"

They drained their glasses and made their way towards the exit. The barman bid them a cheery farewell.

———

Sprocket and Spindle were playing a board game in the lounge and Mrs Bikie and Aunty Agnes were clearing away the dishes from the kitchen table.

"You're late!" said Mrs Bikie scornfully.

"I know," said Mr Bikie, "sorry about that! But we've found out a lot more than we expected to down at the tavern. We've got a lot to tell you!"

"Sounds interesting," said Aunty Agnes, "taking the casserole back out of the oven and placing it on a tablemat in the centre of the kitchen table.

Mrs Bikie helped Aunty Agnes to serve up the veg and potatoes before taking a seat at the table.

"Well?" she said, "Spill the beans. What have you found out?"

Mr Bikie told them all about the two fishermen and the incident at the bar.

"That'll be the McAlister brothers," said Aunty Agnes. "They have a boat called the *Creel Pot*."

"The *Creel Pot*," said McTavish sitting up. "That's what they said. We heard one of them say they would be close to the *Creel Pot*."

"There have been rumours around here for some time that the brothers are having some financial difficulties," said Aunty Agnes. "They took the boat over from their father, Jock McAlister, last year when he retired. But the fishing around here has been bad recently. Some folks say that if Jock were ever to find out how bad things really were it would finish him off. The brothers have managed to keep him in the dark up to now. Even though. I'm surprised that those boys would get themselves mixed up in something like this!"

"They also mentioned something about the *Herring House* and the *Cellars*," said Mr Bikie.

"Well," said Aunty Agnes, "the *Herring House* is at the head of the harbour, and the *Cellars* are what the locals call a series of caves that have been cut into the headland at the bottom of the harbour road. In the olden days they were used to store fish, but it's well known that they were once used for smuggling as well. You access the caves through a tunnel that has been cut into the headland between the harbour and the beach. The tunnel is still used, but the *Cellars* were sealed off years ago."

"Sealed?" queried Mr Bikie. "In what way are they sealed?"

"A heavy steel door has been put into place about three-quarters of the way along the tunnel. It was sealed off before I moved down here from Edinburgh, so I've never actually been able to see inside. It's my understanding that the cave system is quite extensive though."

"They said they would be sailing on the tide. Do you have any idea what time that might be?" asked Mr Bikie.

"I can tell you exactly," said Aunty Agnes standing up and making her way over to one of the kitchen drawers. She produced a booklet and studied it for a while.

"The next high tide is tonight," she announced, "or at least early tomorrow morning, at four o'clock."

Mr Bikie looked at his watch. "It's almost midnight now. We have to do something - I'm going to get Lockum out of there!"

McTavish stood up.

"And I'm coming with you laddie."

"No," said Mr Bikie. "I go alone!"

CHAPTER 22

THE CELLARS

Darkness had fallen and the storm had brought with it heavy rain. Water streamed down his face as he followed the cliff path towards the village. He zipped up his jacket as far as it would go and battled on through the driving rain. Eventually he reached the edge of the village.

Aunty Agnes had told him that the harbour could not be seen from the main road and that he should look out for a large metal swing gate that lay across the track that would take him down the side of the cliffs and on to the harbour front. He found the gate easily and passed through.

The track dropped steeply and as he neared the bottom he could just make out the silhouette of the *Herring House*. In the harbour beyond, a number of boats were bobbing around jauntily, safely hiding away from the storm.

As Aunty Agnes had told him, just short of the harbour front, he found a tunnel cut into the base of the cliff. He took refuge, relieved to be out of the storm. Water dripped down from the tunnel roof and in the distance, at the far end of the tunnel he could hear the sound of the sea crashing against the shore. He flicked on his torch and headed deeper. With every step the sound of the sea grew louder, echoing off the walls as the huge waves picked up shingle and crashed it down further up the beach. Small pebbles then clattered into each other as they scurried back to the sea.

He stopped short when he reached the steel door that marked the entrance to the *Cellars*. The door was no longer sealed but slightly ajar. He pulled it open gingerly and headed deeper into the warren of caves. After a short distance he could hear the sound of raised voices echoing down the tunnel, and eventually he saw a light shining up ahead. He turned off his torch and proceeded cautiously until he was outside the cellar where the voices were coming from - he could hear their words clearly now.

"Put that shotgun away brother. You told me that we were just going to take him out to the rendezvous point. You never said anything about killing him!"

"You don't get that kind of money for nothing little brother and you know we need the money!"

"To hell with the money," protested his younger brother. "I'm not committing murder just for the sake of a boat. The boat can sink for all I care!"

Mr Bikie took a deep breath and stepped out of the shadows into the light. He could see Lockum sitting on a stone bench that had been cut into the wall at the far end of the cellar. Lockum stood up, straining against his chains, snarling like a wild beast - his eyes were full of hatred.

"Here for the execution then, are you Bikie?" he snarled. "I wondered when you would crawl out from under your stone!"

"Who the hell are you?" asked the eldest of the McAlister brothers, swinging round and pointing his shotgun directly at Mr Bikie.

"Von Heinrich sent me," said Mr Bikie in a commanding voice. "There's been a change of plan. The rendezvous has been set back until midday tomorrow. And Von Heinrich told me to take care of him for you." He gestured towards the snarling Lockum.

The McAlister brother kept pointing his shotgun at Mr Bikie looking confused, but Mr Bikie added quickly.

"Oh, and don't worry about the money. Von Heinrich says you'll get the full amount!"

"Suits me," the younger brother said getting up to leave. He turned to his elder brother. "You coming or what?" Mr Bikie continued to speak.

"Oh and leave that shotgun," he commanded. "I'll be needing it!"

"You'll need these as well," said the elder brother, laying the shotgun down on the table and unclipping a bunch of keys from his belt-buckle. He threw the keys down beside the shotgun.

"I couldn't have done it anyway!" he said before following his brother out of the cellar.

"Wait for me!" he shouted after him.

Mr Bikie waited until he could no longer hear their footsteps then walked over to the table and picked up the keys. Inwardly he was breathing a huge sigh of relief.

"Well it's just you and me now Lockum," said Mr Bikie picking up the shotgun. "After what happened last time, I think we'll just leave those chains on for now."

Mr Bikie undid the padlock that shackled Lockum to the cellar wall but left his other chains in place. He waved the shotgun to indicate that Lockum should walk ahead and the two men left the cellars.

The storm was still raging outside and the rain lashed their faces as they made their way up the cliff path towards Aunty Agnes's house. Mr Bikie knocked loudly on the front door and Aunty Agnes opened it to let them in.

"Come on in gentlemen," said Aunty Agnes pleasantly. "I'll put the kettle on for you. You both look as though you could do with a nice cup of tea. Take your visitor through to the lounge please MJ. I've lit a fire through there for you. It will be nice and cosy and your clothes will soon dry out."

Mr Bikie escorted his bemused prisoner through to the lounge and sat him down next to the fire. As a precaution he tethered him to the chair to make sure that he was going nowhere.

"I'll be back!" he said to the very confused looking Lockum.

When he entered the kitchen he found McTavish and Mrs Bikie sitting at the table. Aunty Agnes was busy at the stove brewing up some tea. He placed the shotgun on the kitchen table and took a seat.

"Where did you get that from laddie?" asked McTavish eyeing the shotgun.

"One of the McAlister brothers had it," replied Mr Bikie and he told them the entire story.

"So what have you done with Lockum?" asked McTavish.

"He's in the lounge," said Aunty Agnes, "I'm just taking him a mug of tea."

"I'm afraid I've had to leave his chains on Aunty Agnes," said Mr Bikie. "He still thinks I'm part of the Von Heinrich gang and he's a bit unpredictable at the moment."

Aunty Agnes left the kitchen and came back a few seconds later still holding Lockum's mug of tea.

"He's fast asleep," said Aunty Agnes. "The poor man must be worn out. He looks as though he's had a bad time of it!"

"We'd better call the police," said McTavish, "and tell them that we've got him."

"No wait!" said Mrs Bikie. "I thought we came here to get the treasure. If we hand him over to the police now, he'll try and have us arrested. It could take days to sort it all out, and in the meantime, the treasure will be long gone."

"I know we came down here to get the treasure," said Mr Bikie, "but we found Lockum instead, and McTavish is right, we have to hand him over to the police. We can't keep him here as a prisoner. That would be absurd!"

"Maybe not," interrupted Aunty Agnes. "He's fast asleep at the moment, isn't he? He probably won't wake up until the morning, and in the meantime, he'll be none the wiser."

"That's right," said Mrs Bikie, "the McAlister brothers said they were sailing with the tide at four o'clock. It's almost that time now. You and McTavish could take their place and meet up with the sub at the rendezvous point as planned."

"And then what?" asked Mr Bikie. "Von Heinrich would recognise us right away. It would be a suicide mission."

Mrs Bikie gave it some thought.

"He wouldn't recognise me though would he? Suppose I take the helm?"

"You?" said Mr Bikie.

"Yes," replied Mrs Bikie, "why not? We came here to get the treasure didn't we?" Let's do just that. Let's go and get McTavish's treasure!"

Mr Bikie sat back in his chair and gave it some serious consideration. "Maybe we could pull it off!" he said, a plan forming in his head.

"Excellent!" said Aunty Agnes. "I'll make you a flask of tea and some sandwiches to take with you. And don't worry about Lockum; he'll be asleep for hours. We can hand him over to the police first thing in the morning. With any luck he won't even realise that we've kidnapped him."

CHAPTER 23

THE RENDEZVOUS

"I'll take her out," said Von Heinrich, as they prepared to leave the harbour. Weasel settled down next to him in the co-pilot's seat.

"How long will it take us to reach the rendezvous point?" asked Weasel, studying the radar screen on the consul in front of him.

"In this thing about two hours," replied Von Heinrich. "All being well we will rendezvous with the *Creel Pot* on time and on schedule." He glanced at his watch. "They should have dumped Lockum's body over the side by now."

"Fed him to the fish," sniggered Weasel. Weighed him down, just like you said, never to be seen again!" He laughed hysterically. "You should have let me kill him. It would have been my pleasure."

"It's already smelly enough down here with you without dragging dead bodies around!" replied Von Heinrich. "The McAlister brothers will take care of Lockum."

"You know," said Weasel thoughtfully, "we've got the treasure right - all of it! Suppose we don't meet up with the boys in Denmark? Suppose we head for Norway instead? That way we can keep the treasure all to ourselves - cut them out completely!"

"You're a sleazebag Weasel," said Von Heinrich. "You have no moral compass."

But unknown to Weasel, Von Heinrich had already arranged to do just that - arrangements that would see to it that the rest of the gang would never reach Denmark and never see their share of the treasure. He had plans for Weasel too. Nobody was going to take a share of his treasure - he would see to that!

"When we're done," asked Weasel probingly, "will you let me kill the McAlister brothers for you?"

Von Heinrich looked across at Weasel, his cold grey eyes falling onto Weasel's twisted face. He studied him for a moment and looked straight into his soul. And he liked what he saw. Evil... pure unfettered evil. He would let this one live for now!

"Yes," replied Von Heinrich.

———

The storm still raged as they stepped out of Aunty Agnes's house. They followed the path to the garden gate then out onto the makeshift car park.

"I'll just get my bike from the back of Bertha," said Mr Bikie, heading off across the carpark.

Mrs Bikie and McTavish waited patiently for him to retrieve his bike.

"What do you need that for laddie?" asked McTavish on his return.

"Oh, you never know," said Mr Bikie, "it might come in useful."

"I can't imagine how?" said McTavish.

Mr Bikie looked over to Mrs Bikie. It was then that they realised that they could not take McTavish with them.

Thankfully, the rain was starting to ease and as they approached the *Herring House* the storm had all but subsided.

"That'll be the *Creel Pot* over there," said McTavish pointing through the twilight to one of the larger boats moored along the pier.

They followed the harbour round until they reached a point where a wooden ladder hung over the side and down to the *Creel Pot*. Mrs Bikie swung herself round and started down the ladder. Mr Bikie lifted his bike over his shoulder and followed her. He paused as McTavish prepared to follow them.

"I'm afraid you can't come with us McTavish," said Mr Bikie looking up at him. "It's too dangerous and Von Heinrich will recognise you!"

"He'll recognise you too laddie," said McTavish. "What's the difference?"

"The difference is that I have to go - you don't. I can't let Marion go alone. You can help by casting off the mooring ropes for us, and then get back to the house to look after the others."

McTavish watched as Mr Bikie continued down the ladder. He felt terribly dejected.

Once on board they entered the wheelhouse and Mr Bikie pushed his bike down a short flight of stairs which led to a storage area below.

Mrs Bikie called down after him from the helm.

"I can't find the key to start her. It's not in the ignition."

"It'll be hidden up there somewhere," called back Mr Bikie. "Most boat owners leave a spare key around the place somewhere."

"Well not this one," replied Mrs Bikie rummaging around in the cupboards.

"If we can't find the key," said Mr Bikie coming up from below. "We're going nowhere!"

McTavish called down from the pier. "Having trouble down there are we laddie?" he enquired.

Mr Bikie popped his head out of the wheelhouse door. "There's no key," he called back, "and we can't start the engine."

"I'll soon sort that out for you laddie," said McTavish, swinging his bad leg over the side and starting down the ladder. He entered the wheelhouse.

"Do you by any chance have a screwdriver handy laddie?"

"I saw one earlier," said Mrs Bikie, reaching into one of the cupboards. "Here we go." She handed him the screwdriver.

McTavish knelt down below the helm and carefully removed a metal panel to reveal a circuit board along with a tangle of multi-coloured wires. He started to pull wires out, seemingly at random, before crossing two of the wires together. A whirring sound came from the engine room as the starter motor kicked in and after a couple of splutters the engine roared into life. McTavish stood up looking very pleased with himself.

"I'm the only one here that knows anything about fishing boats," he said. "And what's more. I'm the only one that knows anything about submarines. I can be of real help to you. You have to take me with you. You can't just leave me here."

Neither one of them replied. It was true that they didn't know the first thing about submarines, but they also knew that they couldn't take McTavish with them. Their plan involved using their bike.

"No, I'm sorry McTavish," said Mr Bikie, "you can't come with us."

"Why not?" demanded McTavish angrily. "It's got something to do with that damned bike of yours, hasn't it?" he said accusingly.

Mrs Bikie shot a look over to her husband as McTavish continued...

"It's some sort of machine, isn't it? You didn't have it the night you stayed with me in my croft, and then suddenly in the morning it appeared. Found it you said! And there's more. I've been puzzling over this for some time. How did you manage to arrive at the monastery so quickly? And for that matter, how did you manage to escape from the Loch Ness Monster when it attacked you down there in the lake?"

Mr Bikie looked over to Mrs Bikie and this time she nodded to him in resignation.

"Okay," said Mr Bikie, "we'll tell you. But you have to promise that you'll keep it to yourself. Promise us that it will not go any further."

"I'm a past master at keeping secrets laddie. You have nothing to fear from me. So what do you say laddie - am I coming with you or not?" He reached out his right hand, "Are we still partners laddie?"

Mr Bikie took his outstretched hand and shook it warmly. "Welcome aboard McTavish," he said, "of course we're still partners!"

Mr Bikie left the wheelhouse and climbed up the ladder onto the pier. Secretly he was pleased that McTavish was coming with them. He felt safe in the knowledge that McTavish would stay true to his word and tell no one.

He released the mooring ropes that bound the *Creel Pot* to the pier, and then retraced his steps to re-join the others in the wheelhouse. Then the *Creel Pot* and its buccaneering crew passed through the harbour gates; out into the open sea, and onwards to whatever uncertain fate awaited them!

"So what's our heading?" asked Mrs Bikie from the helm. "Where do you think the rendezvous point with Von Heinrich and the sub is going to be?"

"I saw a chart downstairs," said Mr Bikie, "I'll just go and get it."

He returned a minute later clutching a chart which he spread out for the others to see. Mrs Bikie reached into the cupboard above the helm and produced a box of nautical instruments. She handed them over to McTavish.

"Now, if I remember correctly," said McTavish, reaching into the instrument box and taking out a pair of dividers and a pencil. "One of the McAlister brothers said that they were meeting Von Heinrich and Weasel two miles offshore. If the sub is coming down here from Dunbar, then by my reckoning, the rendezvous point should be somewhere around here." He put a cross on the chart with his pencil.

"How long do you think it will take us to get there?" asked Mrs Bikie.

"Not long. Less than an hour I'd say."

Mr Bikie looked over to Mrs Bikie.

"I just hope our plan works. I'm not happy about leaving you all alone when we rendezvous with that sub."

"I'll be fine," said Mrs Bikie. "Anyway it'll only be for a few minutes. We just have to keep our nerve and follow the plan. You just concentrate on getting hold of that treasure."

"So what is the plan anyway?" asked McTavish.

"We're going to hijack the sub," said Mrs Bikie.

"Hijack it?" said McTavish looking at her inquisitively. "I'd sort of figured that bit out, but how exactly are we going to do that?"

"We're going to go over to the submarine on my bike," said Mr Bikie. "Both of us now! We'll hide below deck and then transfer over to the sub as soon as Von Heinrich and Weasel set foot on the *Creel Pot*. Once we've secured the submarine, I'll come back here and get Marion out."

"I see a problem with that," said McTavish. "If we're both down there under the wheelhouse, and Marion is up here on deck, how are we going to know when Von Heinrich and Weasel have left the sub and are on the *Creel Pot*?"

"McTavish has a point there," said Mrs Bikie. "What about I leave the wheelhouse door open so that you can hear what I'm saying? Suppose we set up a keyword – a sort of password - to alert you that Von Heinrich and Weasel are both on deck?"

"How about 'it's a nice day' or 'it looks like rain'," said Mr Bikie. Something like that?"

"Aye that's a good one laddie," said McTavish. "What do you think Marion?"

"Yes, that's perfect. I'll just say something about the weather and you'll know that it's time for you to get going!"

They all agreed to this plan.

As they made headway the early morning sun cast its first colourful rays across the horizon, chasing away any remnants of the previous night's storm. Another scorching summer's day lay ahead of them and the *Creel Pot* made good progress.

"You two had better go below," said Mrs Bikie. "That sub could appear at any moment now!"

As McTavish had predicted, less than an hour out to sea, the turret of the submarine broke surface a few hundred metres to their starboard side.

"They're here!" called down Mrs Bikie from the wheelhouse, her voice full of tense excitement. "They're about a hundred metres away now and closing fast."

She eased the throttle into reverse, bringing the *Creel Pot* to a controlled stop before heading out on deck to meet them.

The submarine glided to a halt and Weasel appeared on the turret. He climbed down onto the submarine's outer deck and threw a coil of mooring rope over to Mrs Bikie. She grabbed hold of it and pulled in the slack before tying it to the boat's rail. But as previously planned, she used a slip knot to secure the rope. Weasel jumped over and landed on the deck.

Von Heinrich emerged from the submarine and stood on the turret observing Mrs Bikie dispassionately. She became aware of his presence and as his cold grey eyes pierced straight through her - she felt the first seeds of fear and struggled to compose herself. Von Heinrich climbed down and jumped aboard to face her.

"Who are you?" he demanded, "Where are the McAlister brothers?"

"I'm Marion McAlister," said Mrs Bikie shakily. "My brothers sent me. It's a lovely day, isn't it? "

"That's the signal laddie," whispered McTavish. "Let's see what this bike of yours can do shall we?"

As they left the *Creel Pot* they hadn't foreseen the humming sound that resonated around the boat.

"What was that?" asked Von Heinrich turning towards the wheelhouse. "Check it out!" he ordered Weasel tersely.

Weasel drew out his gun and headed for the wheelhouse.

———

Mr Bikie and McTavish arrived in the cramped conditions of the submarine. McTavish immediately headed for the control room with Mr Bikie following on close behind. McTavish sat down and took the helm.

"Can you pilot this thing?" asked Mr Bikie, peering over his shoulder anxiously.

"No problem laddie," said McTavish, "piece of cake! You go up and close the hatch for me, then get back over to the boat for

Marion. I'll take care of everything at this end."

―――――

Weasel came up from below deck, gun still in his hand.

"There's a storage space under the wheelhouse sir, but there's no one down there."

Von Heinrich turned his attention back to Mrs Bikie.

"So why are the McAlister brothers not here in person?"

"They got into a brawl in the *Smugglers Tavern* last night and were arrested," said Mrs Bikie. "They sent me in their place."

"The fools," said Von Heinrich. "What about Lockum, do you know the plan?"

"Well some of it," replied Mrs Bikie.

"Where is the fuel?" demanded Von Heinrich.

Mrs Bikie's heart stopped. No one had mentioned to her anything about fuel before. She struggled to answer.

"You're lying," said Von Heinrich menacingly, drawing out his own gun and pointing it directly at her. "You are not the sister of the McAlister brothers. Who are you?"

But before Mrs Bikie had had the opportunity to answer, the submarine's engines burst into life and there was a metallic clunk as the hatch cover was slammed shut. Von Heinrich, realising that something was seriously amiss, lost all interest in Mrs Bikie and took a giant leap over to the submarine. He landed squarely on the deck as it pulled away from the *Creel Pot*.

Weasel watched on in dismay as Von Heinrich clambered up onto the turret and started to fire shots directly at the closed hatch. But the bullets just glanced off harmlessly. The slip knot that Mrs Bikie had tied earlier came loose and the remaining rope started to unravel, rasping over the rail into the sea.

It was not just the rope that was unravelling; their whole plan was falling apart. She had been rumbled by Von Heinrich too quickly and Mr Bikie had not been given sufficient time to come back for her. She decided to take matters into her own hands and launched herself across the deck, shoulder charging towards the distracted Weasel. But Weasel saw her coming and struck her viciously across the face with the heel of his gun. She was sent reeling across the boat, shrieking with pain as she landed heavily on the deck.

Weasel walked over and stood astride his helpless victim. She screamed in terror and covered her face as Weasel pointed his gun directly down at her. He sniggered, savouring every moment before he killed her. But as he was about to commit this unspeakable act, Mr Bikie flung open the doors of the wheelhouse and charged towards him.

Weasel swung round at the last moment and his eyes widened with astonishment as he recognised who it was. Mr Bikie grabbed hold of Weasel's gun arm and forced it skyward. Shots rang out as the two men fought desperately for control of the weapon. The stakes were high; neither of them could afford to lose!

Mrs Bikie concussed but still conscious, barrel-rolled across the deck towards the fighting men. She grabbed the tail end of the fast disappearing mooring rope and looped it around Weasel's ankle.

Weasel looked down in terror as she continued to wrap the rope round and round but Mr Bikie held him fast until the rope had whittled away to nothing. When it reached its end, Weasel was lifted up in the air and catapulted over the side, screaming like a crazed daemon. They watched as he was dragged off behind the submarine, skimming across the water, desperately trying to free himself. Beyond him they could see the submarine going into a dive.

Von Heinrich clung on defiantly but he was no match for the force of the sea. His grip failed him and he was washed over the side, narrowly missing being chopped up into little pieces by the churning propellers.

Weasel managed to free his leg and started to swim back towards the *Creel Pot*, but Mrs Bikie ran to the wheelhouse and pushed the thruster forward as far as it would go while Mr Bikie cut loose one of the emergency life rafts and launched it over the side. It burst open and self-inflated as soon as it hit the water.

Mrs Bikie re-joined Mr Bikie on deck and they watched as Von Heinrich and Weasel unceremoniously clawed their way onto the life raft.

"I'm not going to do that again!" said Mrs Bikie.

"Oh I don't know," said Mr Bikie. "I thought it went rather well."

"Let's just get out of here shall we."

Mr Bikie nodded in agreement.

CHAPTER 24

THE TREASURE

The sun scorched the deck of the *Creel Pot* as she chugged sluggishly towards land. Once they had covered sufficient distance Mr Bikie cut the engine and Mrs Bikie threw the sea anchor over the side.

"We'd better call the coast guard and tell them to pick those two up," said Mrs Bikie.

"Yes," agreed Mr Bikie, "and we'll have to tell them about Lockum and the McAlister brothers. We'll tell them that Lockum is safe and have the police meet us down at the harbour front when we get back."

"We will have to face some awkward questions when we get back," said Mrs Bikie. "But we have to protect the secret of our bike!"

"I know," said Mr Bikie, "but what are we going to tell them? I mean about the submarine and how we captured it?"

"That's a tricky one!" replied Mrs Bikie. "It's okay to tell them about how you got Lockum out of the *Cellars*. After all, you didn't need to use your bike for that. But the submarine and the treasure, that's a different matter altogether."

They paused for a while to consider their situation.

"I've got it," said Mrs Bikie. "McTavish is the only one that knows how we did it. Von Heinrich and Weasel won't talk, and anyway, they have no idea how we managed it either."

"What about Aunty Agnes?" said Mr Bikie, "She knows we're involved?"

"Don't worry about Aunty Agnes," replied Mrs Bikie, "If I speak to her, she won't say anything we don't want her to. I think she's an old hand at that sort of thing anyway."

"That just leaves the coastguard," said Mr Bikie, "If we radio through to them now they will know that someone other than McTavish was aboard this boat!

"Not if you pretend to be McTavish when we radio through," said Mrs Bikie. "That way it'll be as though we were never here; we never existed in the first place."

"Do you think that McTavish will be okay with that?" asked Mr Bikie.

"I don't see why not," she replied, "after all it'll be him that gets all the praise for single-handedly seizing the submarine. Not to mention bringing the treasure back!"

"Yes I guess that's true," said Mr Bikie. "That's it settled then. I'll call the coastguard, and then we'll get over to the sub and join McTavish."

After alerting the coastguard they went below and sat astride their bike. There was a flash of light and they left the *Creel Pot* to bob around aimlessly in the crystal clear blue sea.

———

McTavish looked up in wonderment as they materialised in the cramped confines of the submarine.

"That's quite a party trick you've got there laddie. I didn't realise that teleportation existed yet."

"It doesn't," said Mr Bikie, as they dismounted their bike, "well at least not as far as the rest of the world is concerned."

"McTavish!" said Mrs Bikie, "There are a few things we need to discuss with you before the submarine reaches port. We'll all have to be singing off the same hymn sheet when we get back - if you know what I mean!"

"I'm listening," said McTavish.

But McTavish wasn't really listening. He kept looking back down the control room to where a heavy metal box lay on the deck.

"I don't mean to be rude lassie," said McTavish, "but can it wait for a moment? If it's all right with you lassie, I'd like to cast my eyes on that treasure back there. I've waited a long time for this moment!"

Mrs Bikie smiled at McTavish. "Yes of course," she said, "I think we should all do just that!"

Mr Bikie nodded in agreement. "Yes!" he said. "Let's have a look at the loot shall we?"

McTavish flicked a few switches and put the submarine into autopilot before they went back and gathered around the very plain looking metal box.

"It's your privilege McTavish," beamed Mrs Bikie, gesturing for him to open it.

McTavish knelt down and slipped off the padlock that hung loose in its clasp. He pushed the heavy lid open and it clattered backwards onto the hard metal deck. The contents of the box were revealed for all to see. Diamonds, rubies, emeralds. All shimmering and glimmering in the unearthly light of the submarine.

McTavish looked down in awe. "It's greater than anything I could have imagined!" he exclaimed. "It must be worth a fortune!"

"Tens of millions," said Mrs Bikie kneeling down beside him and picking out a diamond as big as a golf ball. "No! Hundreds of millions!" she said, twirling the giant diamond around in her fingers.

"McTavish," said Mrs Bikie looking at him earnestly, "there's something we need to tell you! Earlier when we were on the *Creel Pot*, we radioed the coastguard and we had to pretend to be you."

"Why would you do that lassie?" asked McTavish.

Mr Bikie answered the question for her. "Because we can't let it be known that we were ever here. We can't have our bike mixed up in this. There would be too many awkward questions to answer. And there's something else. We are forbidden to make use of our bike for our own personal gain. The treasure...it's all yours McTavish! We cannot take a penny of it!"

"Don't be silly laddie," said McTavish dismissively. "The reward money for finding this treasure is going to be astronomical! We're partners aren't we? There's plenty enough for us all. As far as I'm concerned half of this is yours."

"No McTavish," said Mr Bikie firmly, "we can't take any of it!"

"Are you sure about this laddie?" said McTavish looking at him in puzzlement. He turned towards Mrs Bikie. "Is that what you really want?"

"Yes. That's what we really want," confirmed Mrs Bikie.

McTavish closed the box and returned to the helm.

"We'd better get going," said Mr Bikie looking at his watch. "We need to get Lockum down to the harbour."

They straddled their bike ready to go.

"We'll see you back in Cove," said Mrs Bikie.

And with that they were gone.

CHAPTER 25

THE HOSTAGE

As they entered the back door of the kitchen, Aunty Agnes was busy tidying away the last of the breakfast dishes. She looked up.

"Ah there you are dearies," she said. "You've just missed your breakfast but I made plenty and I've kept some back for you. Now sit down and tell me everything that's happened. I'll put the kettle on; tea or coffee?"

"Coffee for me please Aunty Agnes," said Mr Bikie taking a seat at the table.

"And I'll have tea please Aunty. Where are the children?"

"You've just missed them," replied Aunty Agnes. "They've gone out for a walk with Scottie."

"And Lockum?" she asked, accepting the cup of tea handed to her by Aunty Agnes.

"Oh he's fine dear. I've fed and watered him. He's been no trouble at all really. I think he's trying to befriend me in the hope that I'll let him go," she smiled knowingly. "I've read about that sort of thing in the newspapers you know."

Mr Bikie wondered if Aunty Agnes knew a lot more about such matters than she was letting on, a lot more than just reading about it in the newspapers.

Aunty Agnes continued, "Now tell me everything whilst I plate up your breakfast."

They weighed into a hearty breakfast and recounted some of the morning's events, being careful not to give too much detail - especially anything that involved their bike.

"...and that's what we told the coastguard. So we need to get Lockum down to the harbour front. We've arranged for the police to be down there waiting for us."

"So you and McTavish were able to capture the submarine without Von Heinrich recognising you?" asked Aunty Agnes.

"Yes, we managed to take Von Heinrich by surprise," said Mr Bikie.

"Aunty," said Mrs Bikie, there's something else. We would appreciate it if you would not tell anybody that MJ and I were on board the *Creel Pot* today!"

"But why child, then you'll miss out on your share of the reward money!" exclaimed Aunty Agnes.

"We know that," said Mrs Bikie, "but that is of no consequence."

Aunty Agnes looked at them before she replied. She knew that they didn't have much money.

"I guess you have your reasons," she said. "It will go no further!"

"Thank you Aunty!" said Mrs Bikie.

"You know what," said Aunty Agnes, "I think I'll take Lockum down to the harbour for you. He's getting used to me now, but he reacts very strangely when he sees you MJ."

She looked across the table at him.

"He doesn't seem to like you for some reason, and besides, the local police sergeant is a good friend of mine. I'll smooth things over for you."

"I'm coming with you Aunty," said Mrs Bikie. "MJ can wait here for the children and follow on down when they get back from their walk."

"As you wish dear," said Aunty Agnes.

"Have the children seen Lockum yet by the way?" asked Mr Bikie.

"Oh yes," said Aunty Agnes, "they know he's here. I told them that he was a bad man and that we were handing him over to the police this morning."

"Okay, let's do just that," said Mrs Bikie standing up and getting ready to go. She turned to Mr Bikie. "We'll see you down there shortly MJ."

They left Mr Bikie sitting at the kitchen table. He took a long sip of his coffee, and then leaned back with hands clasped behind his head. He thought about all the things that had happened to him over the last few days. He thought about his first chance encounter with McTavish, of his terrifying ordeal at the hands of the Loch Ness Monster, the sad loss of the *Highland Princess* and the capture of Von Heinrich's submarine. Last but by no means least, he thought about the fabulous treasure he had recovered for McTavish. He started to day-dream about what he would have done with all that money had he been able to keep his share. It had been a hard struggle building up his rescue operation over the years and he had spent every spare penny he had on it.

With a wry smile he took another sip of his coffee.

It was just not to be.

CHAPTER 26

ARRESTED

Sergeant Fergus McPherson watched as Constable Macintyre swung open the metal gate before returning to their vehicle. They trundled down the harbour track with a procession of emergency vehicles following on behind. As they neared the bottom of the track they spotted the McAlister brothers arguing with each other along the pier.

"That's them!" said Sergeant McPherson pulling their police car into the rough gravel carpark on the harbour front.

Sergeant McPherson stepped out of the police car and adjusted the brim of his hat before, accompanied by Constable Macintyre, he walked along the pier towards the McAlister brothers. The brothers looked up in alarm when they saw the two policemen approaching.

"Lost something have we lads?" shouted Sergeant McPherson.

One of the brothers made a run for it, but Constable Macintyre launched himself towards him, bringing him down with a flying rugby tackle. His brother looked on in stunned disbelief as more officers arrived to pin his elder brother down and handcuff him.

"It wasn't us," protested the younger brother, "we haven't done anything wrong."

"That's not what I hear," said Sergeant McPherson. "Where's your boat?"

"We don't know," he replied, "we just came down here this morning and she was gone!"

"That's because she's abandoned and bobbing around somewhere out there," said Sergeant McPherson pointing out to sea.

"Keep your mouth shut!" shouted over his elder brother. "Tell them nothing."

The sergeant continued.

"And not far from your boat the coastguard have picked up two members of the Von Heinrich gang. I don't suppose you know anything about that either, do you?

"We have reasons to believe that the Von Heinrich gang is responsible for the abduction of one of our colleagues, a certain PC Lockum!"

"Don't tell them anything!" shouted his brother again.

"We already know everything," said Sergeant McPherson turning to the elder brother, "and I am arresting you and your brother for the abduction and imprisonment of PC Lockum, a public servant and a member of the Highland Constabulary."

"But we haven't got him!" protested the younger brother. "One of Von Heinrich's men took him away from us last night!"

"We know about that too," said Sergeant McPherson. "PC Lockum is alive and well, and the man who took him away from you will be joining us here at the harbour shortly."

The brothers looked across to each other, confused. This time the elder brother spoke.

"But this guy last night said that Von Heinrich had sent him, and that he was going to kill Lockum!"

"Not a member of the Von Heinrich gang it seems," said the sergeant. "It looks as though you two gentlemen have been misled."

He turned towards his police officers.

"Take them away!" he ordered sternly.

CHAPTER 27

THE HAND OVER

The fully chained, still very confused Lockum was led down the cliff path towards the village. They reached the metal gate at the top of the harbour road and started down the steep incline. Ahead of them, there were flashing blue lights everywhere. A commotion had broken out on the harbour front and they were just in time to see the McAlister brothers being bundled into one of the police vans. As they neared the carpark, Lockum widened his stride with new found confidence.

"You're in for it now!" he snarled at his captors.

"No. Not at all dear," replied Aunty Agnes. "You still don't seem to understand that we are not the baddies around here! It's us that are saving you!"

"So, why am I still chained then?" demanded Lockum menacingly. "You're all going to go to jail for this! Abducting a police officer is a serious offence and I'm going to make sure that you pay for this - all of you!"

"Now don't be so silly," said Aunty Agnes, starting to tire of Lockum. "I'll have you know that we saved your life last night and that you have Mr Bikie to thank for it. If it wasn't for him you'd probably be fish bait by now. We would have unchained you ages ago if it wasn't for your erratic behaviour. It's your fault you're still chained!"

As they approached the gravelled carpark, Sergeant McPherson walked over to greet them.

"Agnes! How are you?" he asked, greeting her warmly.

"I'm fine Fergus," replied Aunty Agnes beaming at him. She turned towards Lockum. "This is PC Lockum. I understand that you have been expecting him."

"Yes," replied Sergeant McPherson, "but I didn't realise that it would be yourself bringing him down here Agnes."

"I've been looking after him for my nephew MJ. He will be down here shortly with his children."

Lockum, who had been listening to their conversation with disbelief, could take it no longer. He turned to Sergeant McPherson.

"You know these people?" he spluttered. "I want you to arrest them for abducting and illegally imprisoning an officer of the law!"

Sergeant McPherson turned to Aunty Agnes.

"Yes Agnes, why do you have PC Lockum in chains?" he enquired.

"Oh the McAlister brothers did that to him Fergus. Unfortunately we weren't able to unchain him earlier. He's been a bit of a handful," she explained. She rummaged around in her handbag and produced a set of keys.

They were interrupted by the sound of Scottie barking excitedly as he careered down the harbour track towards them with Sprocket and Spindle hard on his heels.

"Ah here are the children and my nephew now," said Aunty Agnes looking back up the track.

Lockum turned to see what was happening and was appalled to see Mr Bikie coming down the road towards them.

"That's him!" shouted Lockum tugging at his chains violently.

"He's the ring leader. Arrest him you fools! Don't just stand there, arrest them all. They're all in on it!"

"Now settle down please Constable Lockum," said Sergeant McPherson firmly. "As I understand it, these people managed to rescue you last night. You've been through a terrible ordeal - it's perfectly understandable that you're a little bit upset."

"A bit upset!" spluttered Lockum. "A little bit upset!"

Sergeant McPherson continued. "We've arranged for an ambulance to be here to take you to hospital. They'll have you checked over. You'll be in good hands. Once you've had a good rest you'll see things differently."

Sergeant McPherson signalled over to the ambulance crew who hurried across the car park to attend.

"I don't need a good rest!" protested Lockum, pulling at his chains, "Where are they taking me?"

"As I just explained," replied Sergeant McPherson, "they're taking you to the hospital. They are here to help you. Now be a good chap and go along with them quietly."

He handed the set of keys over to one of the ambulance crew who ushered the loudly protesting, still chained Lockum into the back of the ambulance. They watched as the ambulance's flashing blue lights disappeared up the steep track.

"Poor man," said Aunty Agnes.

CHAPTER 28

THE RETURN OF MCTAVISH

Aunty Agnes introduced Mr Bikie and the children to the sergeant, who made a special point of thanking Mr Bikie for his daring rescue of PC Lockum.

"The McAlister brothers told us that you took Lockum away from them last night," said the sergeant. "We arrested them earlier when they came down to the harbour to get their boat. You certainly had them fooled - they really thought you were a member of the Von Heinrich gang."

"It was very courageous of my nephew to save Lockum like that, wasn't it Fergus?" said Aunty Agnes.

"It certainly was," agreed Sergeant McPherson, "it wouldn't surprise me if he gets a commendation for this!"

Mr Bikie looked slightly embarrassed. "Oh it was nothing really," he said modestly.

Mrs Bikie turned to the sergeant, "Have you had any news of the Von Heinrich gang?"

"Yes," replied the sergeant. "Two of the gang were picked up by the coastguard; we think that one of them is the leader. The others were arrested at Edinburgh Airport. They were trying to board a plane heading for Denmark, but somebody tipped us off. The coastguard found the McAlister's boat abandoned a couple of miles off shore and they said that some chap named McTavish had radioed them to say he had taken over the gang's submarine. I can't imagine how he managed to do that!"

"McTavish is our friend," said Spindle, who had been listening to the conversation with great interest.

"Yes," said Mr Bikie, "he disappeared last night after I rescued Lockum from the *Cellars*. It wouldn't surprise me if the old rascal hasn't managed to seize the treasure as well!"

"Treasure?" asked the sergeant. "What treasure?"

"Yes, Fergus," said Aunty Agnes. "That's what all this is about! The Von Heinrich gang stole McTavish's treasure! And now it looks as though McTavish has succeeded in getting it back from them."

"There's just one thing that bothers me about all this," said the sergeant, turning towards Mr Bikie. "How did you know that PC Lockum was imprisoned in the *Cellars* in the first place?"

"McTavish and I were in the *Smugglers Tavern* last night," replied Mr Bikie, "and we overheard the McAlister brothers talking about him."

The sergeant's voice took on an official tone.

"So why didn't you phone the police and tell us right away?" he asked searchingly.

"That was probably my fault Fergus," said Aunty Agnes, stepping into the conversation. "In view of the time scale and the seriousness of the situation, I thought we should do something about it right away and get PC Lockum out of there. If we'd waited any longer he might be dead!"

Sergeant McPherson seemed to accept this explanation. He had some prior knowledge of Aunty Agnes's past.

"And this treasure?" said the sergeant, "and this man McTavish? Where do you think he is now?"

"If McTavish has managed to capture the submarine," said Mr Bikie, "he'll be bringing it back here to Cove. We should go up onto the sea wall and look out for him."

The assembled group made their way along the pier, picking up followers as they went. They climbed the stone staircase that led to the top of the harbour's outer wall and sat down with their legs dangling idly over the side. One of the policemen had brought with him a pair of binoculars and he scoured the horizon looking out for any sign of the submarine. But it was Spindle that spotted it first.

"There!" she exclaimed, pointing to a patch of white water a few hundred meters off shore.

"Yes, that's the submarine all right," confirmed Aunty Agnes excitedly, "and look, it's surfacing!"

The submarine slowed as it approached the harbour gates, passing through, and gliding serenely across the harbour towards the pier. The excited group of onlookers clambered down the stone steps and back along the pier. They gathered around the wooden ladder that stretched down to the submarine's deck and watched expectantly as the hatch slowly opened. It clattered over to one side as McTavish emerged. He cast up a mooring rope to one of the waiting policemen then started up the ladder towards them. As he reached the top Sergeant McPherson stepped forward to greet him.

"And you'll be Mr McTavish I assume?"

McTavish drew himself up to his full height.

"Aye that's me," replied McTavish. "Hamish McTavish at your service. I've got something for you. You'll find it in the submarine towards the back of the control room."

Sergeant McPherson signalled for two of his officers to board the submarine. After a few minutes they reappeared carrying the heavy metal box containing the treasure. An officer threw down a thick rope which was tied on to the box before it was hauled up onto the pier. Another officer knelt down and untied the rope whilst Sprocket and Spindle nudged their way to the front of the crowd to get a better look.

"Wow!" said Spindle as the box opened.

"Wow!" echoed Sprocket.

The police officers closed the box and carried the treasure over to one of the waiting police vans. A convoy of police cars followed the van up the harbour road, leaving just the sergeant and his colleague behind.

"Well, thank you once again for your help everybody," said the sergeant. "And you sir," he said turning to McTavish, "You are a very remarkable man."

McTavish wanted to tell him that he was far from remarkable and that it was not he alone who had captured the submarine. But as agreed he remained silent.

Sergeant McPherson and his colleague returned to their car and pulled away up the harbour road.

"Well," said Aunty Agnes as they disappeared round a bend in the track, "that was exciting wasn't it? You really must come and visit me more often. I haven't had this much fun in years!"

They all smiled at her warmly.

"How about a nice cup of tea?" she said. "And some warm homemade pancakes?"

"That would be delightful." replied Mr Bikie.

CHAPTER 29

THE MANAGER

Three months had passed and there was a spring in McTavish's step as he made his way between the staff block and the main building. He entered the hotel and headed for the bar. He had made this trip a hundred times before but somehow today everything felt different. The manager looked up from behind the counter as he entered.

"Ah, I see our useless pot washer has decided to grace us with his presence," he said nastily. "You're late!"

He pointed at the door that led to the kitchen.

"You better get in that kitchen, and I want you to clean it until it's spotless. Spotless you hear! Why are you late anyway? Don't you know the new owners are arriving today?"

"The new owners are already here," said McTavish.

"They've arrived!" exclaimed the manager looking flustered. He stepped out from behind the counter and barged passed McTavish on his way to reception. "Get out of my sight," he growled. "The new owners won't want to see the likes of you cluttering up the place. There are pots and pans piling up in that kitchen. Now get to it!"

After a few minutes the manager returned from reception. McTavish was sitting on one of the high chairs at the bar.

"There's no one there!" he said angrily. "And what do you think you're doing sitting there? I thought I told you to get into that kitchen!"

"I'm the new owner," said McTavish casually.

"You!" exclaimed the manager. He laughed out loud, "You really are crazy aren't you?"

McTavish stood up, and from his coat pocket he produced a set of documents. He walked over and handed them to the manager, then returned to his seat at the bar. The manager examined the documents carefully and as he did so his face went pale.

"You really are the new owner, aren't you?" he looked shaken.

"Yes!" replied McTavish. "And I'm sorry to tell you that I have no need of a manager anymore – but you're in luck. I understand that a vacancy has just arisen in the kitchen. Perhaps you would be interested in the position?"

The manager's face turned a very strange shade of purple as though he were about to explode.

"Become a kitchen assistant!" he exclaimed. "I'm a manager not a pot washer! I wouldn't work for you," he spluttered, "for... for all the tea in China!" he said lost for words.

"Oh well," said McTavish, "in that case I'm sorry to say that I'll just have to let you go!"

The manager threw the documents across the room angrily, scattering their pages across the floor before storming out of the bar.

McTavish stood up and walked over to his strewn documents. He carefully put them back in order and tucked them away safely into his pocket. Then he walked behind the counter and poured himself a very large glass of whisky. He raised his glass to the heavens and drained its contents. A broad smile crept over his face as he savoured the moment.

CHAPTER 30

NESSIE'S CASTLE HOTEL

Several months later, all was not well in the back seat of Mr Bikie's car.

"Let go! Let go!" screamed Spindle as she fought for possession. "It's not yours. It's mine. I made it!"

"Oh for goodness sake," sighed Mrs Bikie from the passenger seat, "what are you two fighting about now?"

"Sprocket is trying to steal my card," said Spindle, "and it's not his - it's mine! I made it!"

Sprocket protested.

"I just wanted to sign it and wish McTavish all the best on his engagement. But she won't let me!"

"Well, it's Spindle's card," said Mrs Bikie. "It's up to her if she wants you to sign it or not."

Sprocket slouched back in his seat and made daggers with his eyes at Spindle.

"How long until we get there?" asked Spindle, hiding the card away by her side.

"About another hour," said Mr Bikie. "McTavish and Beth have laid on a special lunch for us and we're going to be his guests for the weekend."

"I hope it's going to be as exciting as the last time we were at Loch Ness," said Sprocket.

"I hope not," chuckled Mrs Bikie, "I don't think I could go through all that again!"

"I'm looking forward to seeing McTavish again," said Spindle. "I told you that Beth fancied him, didn't I!"

"You did not," protested Sprocket.

"Yes I did," said Spindle.

"No you didn't."

"Oh for heaven's sake," sighed Mrs Bikie.

An hour later they pulled off the main road in Drumnadrochit. A large new sign at the bottom of the hotel's driveway read, *Nessie's Castle Hotel*. As they drove up the newly resurfaced driveway, they looked out onto beautifully manicured lawns that stretched down to a fountain, vigorously pushing jets of water high into the morning sky.

They all piled out of the car excitedly when they reached the carpark. At the top of the granite staircase, a new sign above the entrance read, *Proprietor and Licensee Holder, Mr Hamish McTavish*.

They passed through the main door and entered a fabulously refurbished main hallway with tapestries adorning the walls and a red carpet running along the middle of a solid white marble floor. Elegant marble statues had been placed on either side along its length. At the end of the hallway they were greeted by a smartly dressed young lady sitting at the reception desk.

"Welcome to *Nessie's Castle Hotel*," she said smiling at them pleasantly. "Have you booked?"

"I believe we are expected," replied Mr Bikie. "Mr and Mrs Bikie and family."

"Ah, Mr McTavish will be delighted to hear that you have arrived safely sir. He's serving behind the bar at the moment, but he's reserved the *Royal Suite* for you - the finest rooms we have in the hotel!"

She picked up and rang a small bell on her desk. Albert the porter appeared.

"Please take our guests and luggage to the *Royal Suite* Albert."

Albert loaded their bags onto a very posh looking porter's trolley and headed for the lift. The receptionist handed Mr Bikie a very large room key.

"Let's go up to the rooms later," said Mrs Bikie turning to the others. "Let's go and find McTavish first shall we?"

"I'll just give the porter a hand with all those bags," said Mr Bikie. "You carry on I'll catch up with you in a minute."

When they entered the bar they hardly recognised the man behind the counter. McTavish looked resplendent. He was wearing full Scottish dress, complete with a tartan kilt and an immaculately tailored tweed jacket. His beard had been trimmed, and his hair was combed back and perfectly styled.

Beth emerged through a serving door carrying a tray. She gave a cry of delight when she saw them.

"McTavish!" she called over to the bar. "Our guests have arrived!" She breezed passed them with the tray. "I'll be right back," she said. "I'm just taking that gentleman over there his morning coffee."

McTavish stepped out from behind the counter to greet them. Mrs Bikie met him halfway and gave him a huge hug.

"McTavish you look wonderful," she said. "It should be me that is marrying you."

"No you don't," said Beth cheerfully as she returned from serving the gentleman his morning coffee. "He's all mine!"

McTavish looked up in delight as Mr Bikie entered the bar.

"Ah, there you are laddie. Come and have a seat at the bar and I'll get you a drink. There's something I want to discuss with you and Marion."

McTavish accompanied them to the bar and Beth ushered the children away, knowing that McTavish wanted to talk to their parents alone.

"Well children," said Beth, sitting them down at one of the tables, "what would you like to drink?"

"Lemonade for me please Beth," said Spindle. Sprocket nodded in agreement.

Beth returned with two huge glasses of lemonade, complete with a slice of lemon and a cherry on top. The cherry had a little paper umbrella sticking out of it. Spindle giggled in delight as she picked up the tiny umbrella and waved it around in the air happily.

At the bar, Mr Bikie took out his wallet to pay for the drinks.

"Put that away laddie?" said McTavish. "You'll pay for nothing while you're under my roof."

"Thank you," said Mr Bikie. "That's very good of you McTavish!"

"It's not good of me laddie!" said McTavish dismissively. "You know that half of this place should be yours! After all that business down in Cove I'm famous. Folks even believe my story about being attacked by the Loch Ness Monster. Nobody used to believe me in the old days, but now people even ask me for my autograph."

"That's great news," said Mr Bikie, "you've earned it McTavish."

"But it's all thanks to you MJ. I want you and Marion to share in my success!"

Mr Bikie looked dismayed.

"McTavish, we've already explained to you that we can't take any of the reward money."

"Don't be silly laddie. Has it never occurred to you that it was your bike that helped us to recover the treasure? Has it never crossed your mind that your bike might actually want you to have your share of the treasure?"

"Why would it want that?"

"Because," said McTavish, "maybe the bike knows something we don't. Maybe this is just the start of something else. You, me, Marion, perhaps even Aunty Agnes - all of us may be part of something greater. This is what the bike wants!"

"You can't know that," said Mrs Bikie, speaking up for the first time. "If we use the bike for our own reward we may lose the power to control the crystal!"

"As you say lassie," said McTavish, "but I think you are making a big mistake!"

They all fell silent to ponder McTavish's words. McTavish gathered his thoughts and broke the silence.

"I want you to help me!" said McTavish.

"Help you? Help you how?" asked Mr Bikie.

"Look around you," said McTavish. "I've done a lot to this place over the past few months, but this is just the beginning! I'm planning to open a whole chain of hotels just like this one, perhaps even an international chain, and I need someone to help me. Someone I can trust. I'm not asking you to take any of the reward money - I want you to earn it."

"Earn it?" said Mr Bikie. "What do you mean earn it?

"We made a great team you and I laddie. You can't deny that! I would like you to be part of this enterprise MJ. How about it? What do you say laddie? We took on the Loch Ness Monster together. I want you to take on this business with me. What do you say laddie - partners?"

He held out his hand.

"What's daddy talking to Mr McTavish about?" asked Spindle looking over to the bar.

"Oh, it's nothing," said Beth opening the card that Spindle had handed her. "Oh how lovely!" she exclaimed. "Did you make this card all by yourself Spindle?"

"Yes," said Spindle proudly.

"And I see your name is on it too," said Beth, looking across at Sprocket.

"Yes," said Sprocket looking surprised; he looked over to his sister for confirmation.

Spindle smiled at him broadly, and on this occasion, Sprocket returned her smile with genuine affection.

"They seem to have agreed something," said Spindle looking over to where her parents were shaking hands with McTavish. Spindle didn't know why, but somehow she felt that something of great significance had just happened.

Beth followed Spindle's gaze. "That's excellent," she said. "Let's go and join the others shall we?"

The gentleman who had ordered coffee came over to the bar to pay.

"Excuse me for asking," he said, addressing McTavish politely, "but are you by any chance Hamish McTavish, the man that found the treasure and was attacked by the Loch Ness Monster?"

"I am indeed," said McTavish, pulling himself up to his full height.

"I wonder if you would be good enough to let me take a photo of you. I'm writing an article for my local newspaper. I'm sure my readers would be fascinated to read more about you."

"I'll do better than that," said McTavish. "It just so happens that there's another man here that has come up against the Loch Ness Monster." He indicated Mr Bikie.

"Is that true?" asked the gentleman, turning towards him.

"Yes it's true," confirmed Mr Bikie, hoping that he didn't sound as crazy as McTavish had once sounded to him. "I have met the Loch Ness Monster!"

"You may also have heard about my friend here saving PC Lockum from the clutches of the Von Heinrich gang?" continued McTavish. "It was all over the newspapers."

"I helped too!" said Spindle as she joined them.

"Yes," said McTavish. "Spindle is right - everybody in this room has helped me in one way or another. How about we do a group photo, a photograph of us all?"

"That would be splendid," said the gentleman setting up his very professional looking camera. "I'm very grateful to you."

They all lined up for the photo, grinning from ear to ear with pride. But as the gentleman was about to take his photograph, someone else entered the room and walked straight over to Mr Bikie.

"I trust you are well?" he said, offering Mr Bikie his small hand. Mr Bikie took his hand and shook it warmly.

"Wee Johnny!" he exclaimed. "I didn't have a chance to thank you back there in the castle grounds. You do realise that I owe my life to you!"

"That's very kind of you to say so," said Wee Johnny, in his grown-up manner.

Mr Bikie raised his hand to the gentleman as he prepared to take the photograph.

"Wait!" he said. "You have to have Wee Johnny in your photo as well. He's going to be a great explorer one day you know!"

They all lined up again, with Wee Johnny in the centre.

As the gentleman pressed the button on the camera, a shrill voice could be heard calling from the outer hallway.

"Johnny! Wee Johnny! Where are you?"

The End